DATING MIDLIFE DEMONS

A HUMOROUS PARANORMAL WOMEN'S
FICTION

ADEPT AT FIFTY
BOOK 4

HELOISE HULL

CURSING MIDLIFE DEMONS

Stuck in the shadow realm, faced with the truth and straight out of luck. I'm more alone than ever. Even my friends are frightened of me. Happy mid-life to me!

That is, until my demon in rusty armor comes to rescue me.

Now, I realize the magical world is so much bigger than I imagined, and it turns out, bigger than anyone else did, either. The Knights Templar are determined to stage a comeback at any cost, and my star-lit blood is the key to their plans.

With only a demon to guide me, I have to find a way out of the shadow realm and back to Earth before magic is unleashed everywhere—and with it, things more ancient than the Earth itself.

A little snarky, a little epic, and still 100% fun, Cursing Midlife Demons is a PWF adventure novel full of powerful heroines who are aging like a fine wine and finding their place after fifty.

History is merely a set of agreed upon-lies
   - Napoleon

1

The golden orrery whirred, sipping at first, taking what it wanted. My blood. Then, it began to gulp. If I intended on stopping this monstrosity, I needed to summon my strength and do the damn thing now. Death lurked in its shadow, its fingers sliding around my throat, looking for purchase, for a way in. I had to beat Death to his own game.

Already, I was hallucinating. I thought I saw... I swore I saw...

An unbearable lightness took over my limbs, and my eyes doubted their truth.

"Romaine?"

My body threatened to throw up or faint. Perhaps both. Both would work, one right after another.

"Shh, my little bird. I'm here. It's going to be fine."

I shook my head, doing my best to clear it. He was still there. "Romaine, how is this possible?"

"It simply is. Don't ask so many questions. You're dying and will soon be dead if we don't hurry."

"I can feel it."

"Then stop talking."

"How did you find me?"

He glared. Clearly, I wasn't good at taking directions, even under life and death circumstances. Yet, as frantic as I was to get free, I had questions. My blood, flecked with starlight, dripped from my veins. Magic flew from every splatter, hitting realms as it fell. I couldn't even think about what that meant, how much magic was being unleashed. I could only focus on one thing. My would-be rescuer. It was easier than thinking about the other consequences.

At least, that's what I hoped he was. "Is Sophie or Anouk with you?" I asked feebly.

"I came alone. Gallant, was it not?" he said, bowing elegantly at the waist.

I gurgled in response.

"Quite correct," Romaine said, a little chirpy for my taste. "Very gallant. Now, let's get you out of this thing, shall we?"

My head nodded, everything twisting in front of my eyes. I couldn't move. I could only watch the thick, jeweled liquid spill away. I stared at Romaine, my thoughts coalescing and disintegrating almost simultaneously. His face. It was harsher here, even in the dim, nebulous light of the shadow realm. More angular. And his fingers... They had no prints. No whorls or lines like chains, linking him to humanity. He was stripped to his bare essentials here in this place.

My mouth opened slowly, deliberately. "You're a demon."

Romaine didn't look up from where he was examining my bonds. "That is something we'll worry about when you're not lighting up every realm in existence. Probably ones we don't even know about yet. There really are too many to keep count."

"But that's the only explanation. That's what you told me. Only demons and dead things. Unless... are you a strigoi, too? But that can't be, you're not the seventh daughter. Right? Are you a seventh son?"

"Bernadette, you're babbling. Let's focus on the most immediate problem. Freedom. I cringe to imagine how much magic is being unleashed this very moment. Even your world is already being affected, and we won't know the implications until we're back."

I blanched. "My world? Earth... is it changing?"

"Hard to say where the drops have been flung or which realms they have touched. Again, focus, Bernadette. What happened? How were you locked into this contraption? Anything you can remember? Even the tiniest detail may help me free you."

"My father tried to drain my blood to make more magic. He told me about my birth, then he strapped me in. He was some sort of shadow himself. I just... it's too much to take in. My brain can't handle it."

"My little, wounded bird. If there is one thing you don't have to account for in that fascinating brain of yours, it's whether that thing was your father. It was a shadow demon using his image, abusing his memories, and manipulating your emotions."

"But how is that possible?" I asked, my voice soaked in hope.

"I know a demon when I see one. More than likely, your real father was never here."

I recalled the pauses, the considerations. It wasn't my father trying to remember something after being separated from his own reality for so long. It was a monster trying to fake it.

"Shadow demons are simulacrums. Poor representations. Terrible copies. They are enough to fool the hopeful, however, so don't take offense."

Romaine's teeth were too sharp, his canines too long. There was a curl of something in his hair, something hard. Like the sound of his voice. It was all too sharp.

"What?" I blinked.

"You're free."

I twisted my arm in disbelief, and the siphon and straps slid harmlessly to the ground. A light burned at the incision as my skin healed itself, my blood working its magic on itself.

"A simple binding spell, really, but sealed with a memory. Quite powerful stuff, but easy enough to undo once you understand the mechanism."

I opened and closed my fist, feeling pouring back into my extremities like quicksand gurgling down my arm.

"Why did you come here, Birdie?" Romaine's voice was softer now, more as I remembered. His eyes filled with something that could not be demonic, had no place in the world of Hell.

"To save my family. To save my family—and to stop Simon."

"I think you're here hoping to atone. You think by sacrificing yourself, throwing yourself head long into something —maybe everything—dangerous your sins will be expiated by your sacrifice."

"I don't need you to psychoanalyze me—"

"You came to this place of grief and you will be changed by it."

"Changed..." I parroted quietly. I thought of the way he knew how to call that cockatrice's name that first day. How he always seemed to be at Le Maire's side, but knew just enough to stay away when the real danger started. He must have been egging on Le Maire to find the Grail without drawing attention to himself. How he was so coy whenever I asked him who or what he was. How he and Madame Hortense seemed to go way back. Try way, way back.

I could hear Sophie now. If it walks like a demon, talks like a demon, dresses like a demon, it must be a freaking demon. Even his skin had a slight, golden luster to it, as if dusted with fools' gold. What a fool I was. The words slipped from my mouth, my tongue as amenable in this world as my brain seemed to be.

"You don't have to answer. I know you're a demon."

Romaine's body turned so sharp and fast that my non-demonic side couldn't possibly keep up. He had me under his arm and dipped backwards, nearly like a lover, his lips inches from mine. I found nothing familiar in this face that met mine. It was exotic, defiant, otherworldly.

"I always did find you so interesting, my little bird. Good guess, although I wouldn't say it's completely accurate."

I gasped, all of my starlit blood rushing to my head and making me feel very mortal and very, very woozy. I must have been absolutely faint to still find him so damn charming, even as he lied. Or was he? What the actual hell was he? "When we had dinner after Le Maire died, you asked about details you shouldn't have known. You attributed it to Clarette. Then, you didn't say anything about the one I singled out. The Parisian pleasure demon, the ambassador to France. Your chateau is named for pleasure, yet you refuse to kiss me—"

Here, Romaine stopped my rampant speculation, his face swooping close to mine, yet... yet...

"Birdie, there are things you do not understand."

"You're right. I don't understand anything, and what's worse? You know and refuse to help. No, you know what's really worse? You have helped and you haven't. You pick and choose. You save me and then clam up. What the hell?"

"I do what feels good, Birdie. This," and here, he gave me the most lascivious look, "this feels amazing."

"This? No, this feels like you're much too sanguine about our situation."

"Getting yourself stuck in the shadow realm where only the most powerful of immortals dare tread? Child's play for beings such as us. However," and here, Romaine rubbed his chest, still wearing the dapper suit I had become accustomed to when I thought he was a man, an adept or a shifter, but still mortal, "it is quite difficult to exist here. Can't you feel it in your very bones?"

"You make it sound way worse than it is."

"Oh, it is way worse. Not even your father, nor Simon, could physically be here. Only with their shadow demon vessel could they visit this realm."

"How am I here, then? How are you?"

"I am afraid I don't typically answer those types of probing questions. I am a gentleman, after all." Romaine was so casual about all of this that it was hard to reconcile his words with his actions.

"You're joking. This is all a hallucination. I'm dead and this is purgatory."

"No. None of those things are happening. If it makes you feel better, know that I am one of those beings powerful enough to be here. I just chose Bordeterre and France because, well," here he laughed, "I must say I don't enjoy the commute to other Outer Planes, but that doesn't mean it's easy to be here or that we can tarry long."

I looked around me, the golden orrery silent but not broken, the grayscale landscape, the shifting sky. "How can I trust you?"

Romaine laughed, long and loud. I could see the unnatural way he didn't suck in oxygen to catch his breath, and the thought made me shiver. "And you, my little bird? You are not what you appear, either. Or should I call you my little demoness? Should I trust you?"

"I never misled you! I didn't know I had demon ancestry until very recently."

"What a demonic thing to say," he chided, taking my chin between his fingers. I tried to yank away, but he held me fast, his eyes boring into mine. I could find no trace of malice in this creature, whatever he was. Only Romaine.

"Is ignorance a worthy excuse?" he whispered, his voice so low and soft it was hard to determine if his words were a seduction or a threat. Couldn't they be both? Romaine tilted my head back by pulling at the hair along the back of my head, my scalp tingling at his intimate touch. "Perhaps this is a question for later. At this moment, we must leave the shadow realm, quickly. There are other, more *hospitable* realms to continue this discussion."

"I can't go back to ours, yet. I have to find Simon and cut off the head of the Templars."

"A righteous cause, surely, but why put yourself on the line?"

I gave him a scathing look.

Romaine's eyes blinked golden-red for a moment before he composed himself and grabbed my hand. "We must leave this place. No one is meant to be here." Indeed, little patches of skin on Romaine's forearms had begun to flake off. "This place is not meant for anyone, not even the gods. It was chosen that way on purpose."

Slowly, I said, "Does that mean the gods are real?"

Romaine scoffed.

"Fine, Ashavan called them 'so-called gods'. Is that better?"

"Immortals. So-called gods. Idols. Call them whatever you want. In various ways, they have found secrets, and they are not willing to share. This place was chosen during the Colossus of Grief, the orrery made inaccessible for the good of the realms."

"Inaccessible?"

Yet, here we were. I hesitated to leave.

"We must go," Romaine insisted. "Take my hand, Birdie. Trust me."

I paused for effect, but I would be lying if I didn't already trust him deeply, without reservation, whatever he was. After all, he was the only one to find me. To even know I needed finding.

So, I took his hand.

2

The air was clean, but still, I found I couldn't breathe. Where was I? There was a sun, finally, and it was bright; too bright. Tears streaked down my face, and my eyes hurt as I winced. My body felt compacted, my head stuffed with straw.

"Romaine!"

I swallowed and opened my jaw a few times, as if I'd flown by air and just needed to pop my eardrums. The thought made me nearly giggle, hysterically in all likelihood. Where was Romaine? Surely I couldn't be alone, again, already.

"Romaine! I need you," I shouted, my voice less fuzzy.

Romaine's arms scooped me up and held me firmly to his chest, his chin resting on the crown of my head. He was crooning softly under his breath, and the vibrations of his voice soothed me, like a cat's purr, steady and constant. Vibrations had healing properties.

I clung tighter.

"Shh. You're going to be alright, my little bird. You're

going to be fine. We made it out, and we are so very much alive."

I realized a few tears weren't sun-soaked. They were genuine. I was crying. I hadn't even cried at my mother's funeral. Instead, I had accepted it with stiff resolve, just the way she would have wanted. But maybe I should have cried, for me. For Amandine. For a life of secrets with no big reveal.

When I was done, I wiped my eyes on the sleeve Romaine offered and realized he was wearing something else. I looked down. I was wearing something else, too. Gone were the bloodied and torn clothes from the last few days. I flushed in confusion.

"What happened?"

"We are somewhere new. The rules are different. We are different. Come, let's figure out where we are."

I took his offered hand as I examined us. I wore a white cotton dress, simplicity to the max. On my feet were soft tan sandals that molded to me perfectly and made it feel like I was walking on clouds. The only adornment, as far as I could tell, was a single gold band on my forearm. Romaine was similarly dressed, except he had slacks and a button down shirt in place of a dress. Strangely enough, he also had a gold band around his forearm. I clinked them together and smiled like it was some mark, some great joke we shared. With a contented sigh, I leaned my head back and spread my arms.

Great shapes of fluffy meringue-clouds scudded across the blue sky. I could lie on my back in the soft grass and pick out the shapes, dreaming of high seas and krakens or princesses slaying dragons, as I used to do with Amandine when she was a child.

A warm summer breeze came in like a balm after the

shadow realm's mists. It smelled of freshly mown grass and fragrant lavender. The fields were lush and deep. Clover-covered and scented with peonies in full bloom, they wrapped me in a blanket of calm I hadn't felt in ages. I wanted to lie down and roll in them like a colt, to let Romaine lie and roll next to me, too. His fingers laced between mine and held on tightly. In this field with nothing but open vistas before us, it could have felt exposed and dangerous, but on the contrary, I felt more secure. Were they pumping calming pheromones into this atmosphere? Did I care?

No. I did not.

I felt like giggling again, perhaps a tad less hysterically and more like a teenager. With a tug on his hand, I did just that. I dropped and rolled, laughing. It felt wonderful, and a sigh escaped. Intellectually, I knew I had to find and face Simon. I knew my blood had splattered across the realms. Where it hit and how potent the concentration was, I didn't know. There would be time enough to deal with all of those repercussions. Couldn't I have one afternoon, perfect in every way, frozen just for me? Just for a little while?

Romaine's body covered mine as he rolled on top of me, propping himself up on his elbows. His face, unlined except for the barest hint of crows' feet at the corners of his dark eyes, still looked chiseled as if from rock. Living in the South of France meant his perpetual tan made his silver hair quicken in the sun and take a life of its own as it hung between us, his face mere inches away. I watched his eyes dilate and zero in on the pulse at my neck before dragging them up to my lips. I felt my own heart speed up.

"This place is perfect," I said, my heart thudding in my chest. Could he feel my emotions? Guess what I was thinking? It wasn't that deep, really. Lust rarely is.

Romaine nodded. "It certainly is beautiful." His finger-tips danced lightly across my skin.

"Thank you for taking me here, and for always knowing what I need—especially when I'm tied to an ancient machine by a mythical demon of shadows. This is exactly what I needed. A small break before I must find Simon."

Romaine winced, rolling off and flopping in the clover next to me. "You have a one-track mind, even here, in a place designed for you."

"So you know where we are?" I asked, dreamily. I felt drunk on sunlight here, tipsy in the clover. It had to be something in the air to calm me so. I scooted closer so that our cheeks were touching, his skin as warm from the sun as mine, together, two infernos meeting.

"To be quite honest, I'm not sure. You are radiant here, however. That is what I choose to focus on. The sun has blessed you, kissed you with its warmth."

"Kissed?" I asked, my breath hitching.

"Oh yes, practically ravaged."

The long grass tickled my face as Romaine bent toward my neck and kissed it, slowly, languorously. His fingers circled the pulse at my wrist before moving up my arm and over the silhouette of my dress. They stopped to draw little whorls over my breasts, which felt like being shocked with a lightning strike, making me gasp, but he quickly scooped me up and brought me to sit on his lap.

The moment our lips touched, finally, *finally*, it felt like being electrocuted, in a good way. Holy hell, I had never been kissed like this. My entire body pulsed, and I needed to wrap my arms around this man to keep myself stable.

It was, quite simply, a jaw-dropping, heart-stopping kiss to end all kisses. The tingling began at the base of my spine and swept like a wildfire up to my neck. It stormed around my face, stifling any reservations as his tongue found mine. His hands moved to my hair, managing to pull me closer, yanking gently, igniting more little fires and tingles all over my body.

When the real fire came, I wasn't expecting it. Why should I? This was a perfect moment, a perfect summer day. It was hard to compute. My arm was searing and bright, too sudden, too harsh for this soft moment. But then, Romaine was roaring and my screams were high-pitched.

The golden bangles on our arms had ignited together, the metal liquifying into a molten mass on our skin. Then there was space, and the pain was gone, the bangles still intact, and I had to open my eyes to the man before me and come to terms with what had just happened. Because for just a flash, I thought I saw something, something I couldn't associate with the dapper man before me. I saw real fire and even...I blinked. I couldn't understand.

Horns. I swear he'd had horns.

My chest heaved as if I'd just sprinted through the bayou with an alligator in hot pursuit. I put the back of my hand to my mouth for a moment to collect my swirling thoughts, the phantom sting of burning metal was just that—a phantom. The man before me wasn't real; he was, at best, an illusion. A lie. I could ask questions, but would I receive answers?

Romaine was also staring at me strangely, just as confused. He looked from the gold band on his arm to mine. He wouldn't meet my eyes. It didn't sit right. Something didn't sit right.

"Look at me."

He refused.

"Look at me, Romaine."

Still, he wouldn't. I put both hands on his shoulders and pushed him backwards, just to see his eyes. I nearly screamed again when I saw them, my stomach lurching in fear. They were embers, burning red hot. For the first time, I saw Romaine angry. Really and truly angry. With me. His face was still unbearably beautiful, but twisted, like the way a raging sea is terrifying in its raw power and foaming white caps.

"Who are you?" It was a command, and I reveled in making it. It was the only pleasure I could wring from this situation now.

Romaine looked as if for a second he would storm and rage as a true sea would, but then it was gone, nothing but a high passing cloud. "My name is Belphegor."

And then, just like that, with one sentence, it all clicked into place. The executioner's hand never misses, never wavers as it brings down its abattoir judgment. This was no regular demon, strolling where he wanted by mere chance. This was *the* demon. Belphegor of the Le Dragon Rouge. A high-level executive, evil and pleasure incarnate—

"A Duke of Hell," Romaine finished for me. "The Devil's ambassador to France."

And the only thing I could think of to say off the cuff? "Well, I'm not calling you that."

As Romaine laughed softly, tousling the hair at the nape of my neck, it all came rushing at me. Everything had been mouthful after mouthful of lies, and I had lapped them up like a kitten with cream.

"You. You used me. You sidestepped every question I ever asked." My chest knotted, my fingers went cold. "You would have taken me, the first man I've ever had since my husband died, and you wouldn't have even been a man."

"Birdie—"

"Don't call me that. You don't deserve it. I am Madame DuMont to you."

"Fine. Behave like a child, Madame. I don't have much time for your theatrics, and neither do you." I flinched when I heard how cold and informal his voice had grown, how like ice it was now, instead of the fire it had contained only a few minutes ago.

"I don't understand a lot of things in life. I never will. But there are some things you can—and you will—clear up right now." My voice brooked no disagreement.

"I am a demon. What of it? So are you. I tend to stay above the fray if I can, yet I came for you."

"Why?"

"I don't like what I see happening on Earth, and change for humans means change for me. I am offering my help."

My arms crossed over my chest. There were whorls swirling on my skin, like I'd seen in the shadow realm, but then they were gone. I met his eyes, making mine hard as flint. "Did you always know what I was? Before even I did?"

"No."

"Did you sense it?"

"Something odd, yes."

"How long have you been on Earth?"

"A very long time, but not nearly as long as you'd think."

I started to seethe. "If you think you can start to give me ambiguous answers now, you have no idea what I'm capable of."

Romaine moved closer, put his hand to my cheek to thread away pieces of my hair, but paused, his fingers curling into his palm. Here, he was afraid to touch me. I wondered if that meant he could never touch me again or was it just in this place? It was possible no one knew. We were treading on new ground.

"I came at various points, to various places, over the course of human history. At some places, I lingered, like

Assyria. Most, I did not. I must admit, I got lazy. Well," he scrubbed his head with a hand, "lazier. Humans are so very much work. But I stayed for good in Western Europe sometime in the fourteenth century. I recall there being a plague most of the humans were worried about." He shrugged. "It was a long time ago, and the details escape me. Death and disease aren't really my area of expertise."

"What is your 'area of expertise' then?"

"Inventions. Money. Pleasure. Come now. You read about me in your grimoire. I like to make people money, to live out their dreams, so they forget to think about heavenly things. It is so easy to do, which is exactly how I like it. To rest on their laurels and become sloth-like."

I actually turned my back to the charming demon, grinning right next to me. "Well, I still think it's the dumbest deadly sin I've ever heard of."

"You've never met pride," he countered.

"This is not a joking matter, Romaine! You're a damned Duke of Hell!"

I hated the light lilt that was back in his voice. I loathed it. It was too much. We were not friends again. This changed nothing. If he thought for a second he was going to worm his way into my good graces so easily, he was sorely mistaken.

"Don't you get it?" I asked, pain and anger staining my voice. "It was all a game, but only one of us knew we were playing. I didn't know you were demonic; you appeared in the shadow realm like an angel. Why lead me on this chase? Haven't found enough willing virgins for your altar of sacrifice?"

"I haven't had one of those in years."

"What?"

"An altar of sacrifice, and I preferred shiny things at the time. Gold, silver—"

I put up a hand. "Stop talking. That's not helping. Anyways, I want to know why you brought me here. To seduce me and then... What? I have no clue, actually."

"No. You're wrong."

"About which part, exactly?" I snapped. "The seduction, the lies, the game?"

"I didn't bring us here. You did. This time, the game is yours."

3

My anger alchemized into something white hot and furious, burning bright and long. Under the heat of my fury, Romaine's eyes burned, too, and I thought I saw a flicker of enjoyment, even approval. Not fear, like Blaise wore, not worry, like Anouk.

"The moment is ruined," I snapped. "It's time to go."

I let it burn as fiercely as it wanted, and when Romaine put his other hand around my waist, I didn't flinch. Together, we propelled ourselves from this plane and entered another. With a jolt, my feet hit solid ground. I stumbled, but Romaine's arms caught me.

A dark twilight blanketed the land, and my eyes had trouble adjusting at first. It smelled strongly of cypress trees and decay. "Where are we?" I whispered, my mouth fuzzy and full-feeling.

"I believe I know. Come, milady."

"What happened back there? What did I do?" I begged as mist snaked its way around my legs, sentient, or, at least, playing very good at clinging to my body.

"As far as I can tell, you made yourself a safe space. It

must have been instinctual, like a child looking for comfort. They choose things to bring them instant relief. A beloved toy, perhaps. Or their parent. You chose a perfect summer day and forced everything around you to be truthful. The truth is what gives you comfort."

A perfect summer day. Like ones I used to have with my daughter. Of course. And of course the truth gave me comfort. It's why Maman's secrets cut so deeply. It's why they hurt so much more than I expected.

Romaine continued. "In that place, my kiss cost us physically, but I could kiss you now. I could do whatever you wanted me to do to you and things you didn't even know I could." The demon paused, an inscrutable look on his face. " I get the impression that the feeling is no longer mutual. Come, little bird. Look."

"You're correct. It isn't."

Romaine said nothing to defend himself, instead, beckoning me forward toward a stone well. There was a hand crank and a wooden bucket waiting to be dunked. Something swished against my legs as I stepped forward. I looked down. A different dress. How exactly? The lightweight cotton one was gone, replaced with a new, heavier white dress with a gold *cintura* around my waist, looking straight out of a Pre-Raphaelite painting. Glittering sapphires dotted the belt, and a strip of the leather hung to my mid-thigh.

"Romaine?" I asked, realizing he, too, had changed clothing. No longer tailored in a finely woven suit, he wore a black shirt edged with gold thread, that fell open to show off his collarbone and muscular chest, thick with dark hair. A black silk jacket tapered at his waist and ran down to his knees. A thin sword tucked into a scabbard glinted at his belt. From the way his hand casually rested on the hilt, I had a feeling it wasn't just for show. And yet, his costume change wasn't the surprising part. Curving nearly a foot over his head sat a pair of horns made of bronze and devilishly sharp. I guess he wasn't planning to hide his demonic nature in this realm. Wait. What did that mean about me?

With a panicked look at Romaine, I ran to the well and peered into the silvery, reflective water. It was still dark, but I could see my hair braided down my back with gold thread twisted in my graying locks. Two curls hung loosely down each side of my face, and two small horns, barely a thumb's length, peeked out of my hair.

I reached up tentatively. They were short, like a faun's. Nubbins, really, but they were there. My heart thumped harder, my blood pressure skyrocketing.

Demon.

This was the physical evidence, a reminder, a sign, a thing I couldn't escape. I was a demon. My mother had fallen from grace, and she let me live a false life right until the end. She would have let me die, living a lie. Dread dug its claws into my heart. My life would never be the same. I was part demon. Or did the percentages matter? Did even a fraction of demon poison me and make me one hundred percent demon, like one drop of cyanide poisoning an entire well of pure water?

I felt Romaine's presence behind me. He was a full demon, no doubt about that. Romaine was a demon of pleasures and pretty things, and he had lived more lives than I could imagine. His presence shouldn't be a balm; it should be a terror. Anyway, I was still, technically, mad at him.

"Birdie, you are going to be fine. Nothing has changed, except now you know more about yourself and the truth about me. That is a good thing, no?"

"Haven't you heard the saying, 'ignorance is bliss'?" I

muttered, still caressing the silky, velvety horns sprouting from my skull.

Romaine laughed, a deep, melodious sound that was intended to make mere mortals weak in the knees. As for me, it only made mine buckle a bit. "What a very human thing to say, my little bird. Come, let us explore."

"Where are we? And I'm not your little bird. I'm Madame DuMont," I said, sulkily.

"A crepuscular plane where it is easier to exist as we are. Here it is always twilight, the world always half-hidden and yet, half-exposed."

"It sounds like you brought us here with purpose," I said. "Not me this time, right?"

Romaine lifted my chin with his thumb and index finger, forcing me to stare into his brilliant eyes, completely golden and round in this realm. His hair was no longer gray either, no silver fox, but black as ink. It was Romaine, but not. My pulse notched up again as his fingers held me in place, but then he smiled and that dimple appeared—the first thing I'd noticed when he banished the cockatrice at his bistro— and I could exhale.

"I only tried to guide you and your fury, Madame. You are the power behind this. Coming here, what will we find, this is your quest, your purpose. You chose to go to the shadow realm and these are the consequences. Magic was unleashed everywhere. If you want to stop Simon, we begin here."

"I didn't... that's a lot of... accusations," I ended faintly. "Why are you doing this, anyway? Why help me? Finding and crafting a dowsing rod, saving Clarette, hell, even saving me in a shadow realm. Why step in now after centuries of doing nothing, demon of sloth?"

Romaine tilted my chin higher and held it firmly. I

couldn't wiggle away if I tried. By natural means, of course. I could probably try magical means, but I didn't really want to. His touch was still comfort, despite it all.

"I will ignore the end of that, but as I said before. I do what feels good, as all demons do. As you did, did you not? You did what made you feel good by coming to the South of France, trying to save your mother against her will, and then abandoning your friends to go save the world in the shadow realm. That is what demons do. Things that fuel our pleasure. Things that feel *good*."

Angrily, I tried to say something, anything, in my own defense—abandoning my friends indeed!—but Romaine jerked my chin harder, tutting a little. "As for this realm, it houses a white stag. This white stag has horns of gold, and if you catch the beast, you can shave off filings and use those to spark a fire and grant yourself a wish as it flames."

"Like a birthday wish?"

"No, like one that comes true. We can make a wish, and it will tell us where we need to go next to find and defeat Simon."

I blinked. "Oh. Really?"

Romaine let go of my chin to run his palm along the edge of my cheek, his dimple still twinkling, his horns still very much there. I shivered at his touch. "To the woods we fly, little bird."

I didn't bother to correct him. A demon was going to do what a demon wanted to do. "What happens when we find Simon?"

Romaine's grin turned terrifyingly sharp and feral. "We do what one does to all pests. We exterminate him."

* * *

THE WOODS WERE LOVELY, dark and deep. Scratch that, they were just dark and deep. My dress slithered over the wet leaves like silky snakes, and I found it unsettling to walk for hours and have the soft shadows remain unchanged. Neither light, nor dark, the landscape remained dusky. A twilight realm, Romaine had said.

At first, I found myself tongue-tied, then weary and quiet. The hours began to catch up to me, and I caught Romaine watching me too often to count.

"You should rest," he said at one point.

Ignoring that, I bent to the ground, my knees cracking as I looked through the wet leaves for any sign or hooves.

"How do we find this stag?" I asked, up to my knuckles in rot and decay. An earthworm flopped across the back of my hand, and I quickly wiped my hands on my legs. The bottom two inches of my dress were soaked, leaving my ankles damp and raw. It was a thoroughly miserable experience. Cursing the tight bodice and thick dress material I was forced to wear here, I dragged myself to my feet.

"I am not leading you on some merry chase, milady," Romaine said, bowing thinly from the waist. "We have a specific destination in mind."

"Please, be more cryptic."

Maybe it wasn't the smartest move to behave so flippantly around a Duke of Hell, but this was Romaine. It was odd to feel so confident, but I was. I knew him better than that. He wasn't going to bite my head off. For one, he was a demon of sloth. A quick trigger and fast motions seemed like entirely too much work. He did them, on occasion, but not without effort.

"You asked before about immortals. We are looking for one."

"An immortal! Who?"

"She goes by many names, as these types are wont to do. You would probably know her as Nimue or the Lady of the Lake."

We crested a small hill, and I gasped. Out of the twilight rose an enormous castle, except it wasn't tall and full of sharp spires. It spiraled outwards along the ground like the arms of an octopus. Its rays were in the shape of a star, and I could imagine all of the secret passages honeycombed inside, like an apple going rotten, eaten by worms and riddled with dangerous holes.

"The Lady of the Lake lives there?" I asked. "I don't see any water."

"These outlying wings of the castle all radiate from the center, which is a lake. Does that satisfy?"

I held up my hands. "Hey, it's none of my business if it's a misnomer or a deliberately misleading title. Maybe that chicken don't fly."

"As fascinating as I find your habit of speech, I do not believe everyone will be so... mesmerized."

I thought about how his costume change had also made it so he was suddenly allergic to contractions in his own habit of speech, but I didn't say that out loud. Romaine was right about one thing; I was out of my depth here. If he knew better, I'd do well to listen. He had saved me from certain death, after all. And he'd crisscrossed realms and planes he hadn't visited in centuries to do so.

"So," I began, a bit more nervously. "Is Nimue... nice?"

Romaine shrugged, "Depends on your definition of nice, I guess."

"That sounds like hedging to me. Are you saying we should be nervous? Because I just faced down shadow demons. What do I really have to be nervous about anymore?"

"While I admire the confidence, it goeth before a fall. The Lady of the Lake was also known to others as Grendel's mother, a demon, a fiend, a creature of the depths. She is the mother of monsters. She is a water-witch, the only warrior strong enough to take on heroes. She is a king-maker, the one who makes it so. Nervous? Perhaps. On guard? Most certainly."

"Beowulf," I breathed. "The Lady of the Lake from Arthurian legend is also from the epic of Beowulf? I haven't read that stuff since... well a long time. High school, at least. Of course it's real."

"Bien sur, milady." Romaine bowed slightly again.

I gave him a sideways look. "All this courtly courtesy is going to get real weird real quick."

"But one cannot possibly resist while wearing a doublet."

"I'm sure I could."

Romaine ignored my quip, as I assume most gallant knights were taught to do. "Nimue gave Arthur the sword Excalibur, but she also created Beowulf's kingship. That one was... a bit more unintentional."

"What does that mean?"

Romaine paused at the entrance to the castle. "Sometimes, the things obscured by the lakes should stay that way."

"Yeah, thanks for clearing that up. Very helpful."

A pleached archway of white orange blossoms and delicious looking orbs of jewel toned oranges hung over us. The inner courtyard looked incredibly well maintained, as if dozens of gardeners and servants whisked around the twilight hours, pruning and mulching.

I pulled down a plump orange hanging from its branch.

On closer inspection, it had a faint silvery tint, as if kissed by dusk and not by dawn.

"Nimue will join us for dinner," Romaine said. "In the meantime, feel free to freshen up. While this realm scrubbed us clean of all our impurities from the shadow realm, I find it refreshing to do so physically as well."

"You're saying we can march right in and make ourselves at home?"

"Yes, you will find Nimue a most gracious hostess, most of the time."

"And what about the other times?"

"Not so much. But come now, what do you have to fear?"

Considering I'd almost died once in these realms, I figured it was a lot, but Romaine had already entered the stone walls. They exuded a chill and a wetness that seemed unpleasant, but as soon as we turned one of the star corners, a roaring fire met us. It was dozens of steps away, but the warmth reached the whole of the sparsely decorated room.

"I believe there are quarters to your left that would be most suited to you."

"Okay," I drew out, nervous now that Romaine was leaving me alone. "You're sure you've been here before?"

"Oh yes. Nimue has not been on your plane, Earth, that is, for many, many centuries, but I have visited occasionally. We're practically family. Do not worry, little bird. You will be fine. I shall meet you for dinner in an hour. Feel free to wander."

Pulling on a thick iron ring, I stepped inside a room that looked straight out of sixth century Europe. Or, what I imagined it would look like at that time. Everything was so tiny, as if made for people who didn't eat enough fruits and vegetables and who died with their spines twisted from what were now easily curable diseases.

Shaking my head, I tried to wipe death thoughts from my brain. On the damask-covered bed, a simple shift dress lay exposed, and next to the window overlooking the lake was a bathtub made of stone. I walked to the window and peered at this famous lake. Thorny trees dipped their roots at the edges, and frost sparkled among the spikes. I shivered, something primal touching my soul as I peered at it. To be frank, I'd had enough primal shit. I wanted a bath.

Upon closer inspection, water already filled the stone bathtub, and tiny pink cinquefoil petals dotted the surface, mixing with curls of orange peel. It smelled fabulous and fragrant. Now this was what I was talking about! I couldn't wait. My last good soak was ruined by Fabien—wait. How did Romaine know the demon? They had exchanged angry words at Maman's funeral and then Fabien had all but summoned me to UFOPP where he tried to murder me.

No, Birdie, no, I told myself sternly. *You will not ruin another bath because of a demon. Wait until after your bath to ruin things.*

With that settled, I slid into the stone tub and let the heat ease the worst of my aches. Some type of essential oil dotted the surface, the globules skimming past my fingertips when I tried to scoop them up. Just within reach, I found an ewer of wine and on a plate next to it, four tiny, marchpane white hearts that smelled of rose water. Sugar-dusted almonds rested on the silver platter between them. I poured some of the wine and took a bite of the marchpane while I soaked. Simply delicious, although the wine tasted like dark cherries and was a bit sweet for my tastes.

And nothing was ruined, except for the fact that towels weren't a thing. I drip dried as best I could and re-plaited my hair while still wet. It would probably produce nice, waved tresses when I unwound it later, just like all those old oil paintings of the Lady of Shalott. My supposed ancestor. My father—or, my father's memories—remembered he was the Lady of Shalott's descendant through her son, Lancelot, and his ill-fated lover, Guinevere.

I watched myself in the looking glass, my hair braided and wound, my dress low-cut. Something moved in my facial expression, a flicker in the candlelight. I took a step backward. Had I actually moved? Or was it a trick of the light?

A hand wrapped itself around my head, clamping my mouth shut so I couldn't scream, couldn't say the words that would save me. The same feeling of something half hidden that I felt in the shadow realm consumed me, and I knew if I looked up, I would see the wavering image of my father strangling me, holding me high in the air as my legs kicked uselessly back and forth. I managed to reach out and gain one fingertip of purchase on the demon, and for a second, I felt a supercharged power. Even though my mouth was covered and I was voiceless, I screamed anyway, and my voice rang out loud and clear.

Then, there was nothing.

My father was dead and I was alone. A loud wood scraping sound knocked me to the present, and Romaine was standing in my room, concern accentuating the dark shadows of his face.

"Bernadette, I heard a scream."

My entire body felt supercharged, on pins and needles, but there was nothing physical that I could point to in order to explain it. Only shadows playing games, which was the point of the attack. Simon was showing that he could find me and hurt me psychologically. His was a war of games. And they were working. Or, was it all in my mind? I didn't look disheveled, like I had just been in a life and death struggle, even if it only last a few moments. Was it this realm, making me see and feel things that weren't real? It was an alien world, so who was to say?

I rubbed my arms vigorously, hoping to dispel the unpleasant sensation of adrenaline flooding and leaving my body. "It was nothing. Simon and shadows, perhaps. Or I'm just jumpy. Can he reach us here?"

"I would venture to say no, but I do not know for sure. He has command of shadow magic, which has not been done before. Are you quite sure you are fine?"

I smiled again at his sudden inability to form contractions and gave my head a quick jerk yes. After a long look, Romaine nodded. "Very well."

"I'll see you in a few minutes," I promised. "I just need to center myself."

Fifteen minutes later, I met Romaine in a long dining room, the table nearly twenty feet long. Large golden platters arranged with pyramids of juicy, plump fruit sat on either end. He was dressed smartly, still wearing his sheathed sword. Extending a hand, he took my arm, kissed my knuckles and gave me a spin. Thick gold silk could be seen through the slashes of laced fabric in the arms and slits of the brocade. It was still the heaviest dress I'd ever worn, but the feeling of twirling was divine.

"Enchanté," he murmured, his golden eyes burning and his horns nearly scrapping the dinner table when he bent low.

"Will Nimue join us for dinner?" I asked, a little breathless.

"I believe so. But please. Be seated while we wait. Immortals move at a different speed, and while I have gotten used to your schedule and span, I'm not so sure Nimue remembers after all her time here."

I settled in the high-backed oak chair next to Romaine, who sat at the head of the table. Even in someone else's castle, I guess he outranked everyone.

"Why is she alone here? It's so isolating. If she once stood in lakes and gave swords to men, if she once slit throats—still a tiny bit foggy on all of that, by the way—why be here?"

"That is Nimue's business," Romaine said. "Did you feel that?"

Butterflies unfurled their wings in my stomach, but Romaine gave my hand a tight squeeze.

"Are you ready?"

As soon as the words left his mouth, the entire room began to vibrate on a subatomic level. The immortal was coming. And she was powerful.

I dearly wanted to close my eyes and sense her vibrations more fully, but in no world would I leave myself so open to attack. I knew it was a problem to rely so heavily on my physical sight, but it was a fifty year old habit that I was loathe to break.

The vibrations grew heavier, physically so. I had to steady myself on the table, noticing all the while that Romaine merely sat there, a wicked smile curved onto his lips to match his horns.

And then she was there, ringed in turquoise. That was the first impossible thing to notice. After that, she was too brilliant, nearly too much to take in. I settled on focusing on one of her shimmering arms, like fish scales, opalescent and bright. It almost appeared as if she crushed creamy pearls into powder and used them as a lotion.

"Peace, guests, unexpected though you are," a deeply feminine voice said. "Be welcome to this table and my bounty."

Romaine stood, indicating I should, too. Roughly, we pushed back and waited for the immortal witch-woman, the mother of monsters, the maker of kings to sit at the other end of the table.

Nimue had black hair as dark as the deepest trench in the oceans. She let it curl down her back and over each shoulder like waves. She smelled a bit briny, reminding me of the same scent from the Great Lakes. Not as harsh as an ocean brine but still fishy. I had a feeling that sentiment fit her well. Perhaps not as wild on the surface, but just as deadly when roiled.

"I sense you, demoness," Nimue said, spearing a black plum with her nail. "You have human in you, but not any human. A descendant of the Lady of Shalott?"

"Yes. Through my father." Hastily, I added, "Although I have not taken up the mantle of her mission, just yet. I have no allegiance to the Sisterhood of Serpents, nor the Order of Ancients."

"So you waffle."

The little hairs on the back of my neck stood at attention. She was baiting me, like a fisherman calmly hooking a worm and casting it off into the stream. I wasn't sure which was the right course of action. Take the bait or ignore it? A look at Romaine's placid face revealed nothing, so I calmly informed her, "I am still new to this world, and I prefer to collect information first. Then I will analyze all available data and decide upon a course of action. Stinging hearts and misplaced emotions pale in comparison to a well-thought out proposal."

Romaine laughed, splitting the ringing silence at that statement. "In her mortal life, Bernadette used to be what humans call a practitioner of the law. It is in her nature to be cautious. I can hardly fault her for that."

"No, you wouldn't. Although I don't believe your reticence to act is merely out of an abundance of caution, eh, Belphegor?"

Romaine leaned over my hand, frozen near my empty plate. "She is calling me lazy, but in the nicest way possible."

"You are the demon of sloth," I pointed out. "But the nicest demon of sloth I've ever met."

Nimue barked a laugh at that. When she tossed her head back, I noticed a long scar running across her neck, as if she'd survived a botched murder attempt. It was jagged and welt-like, with angry red spots that glimmered and changed as she moved.

"I must agree with Bernadette, a descendent of Shalott. You know I have some history with your forbearer, Elaine."

"Elaine?"

"Why yes. You didn't think 'Lady' was her full name, did you? No, of course not."

"What did you know of my ancestor?" I asked, suddenly more hungry for information than I'd ever been for food.

"They say Elaine died of unrequited love. They say that Lancelot spurned her for Guinevere, even though their doomed love brought the world to flames."

My mouth went dry. What did she mean by 'spurned?' Lancelot was her son, not her lover. "That's not true. Elaine didn't die that way," I said, remembering what the shadow demon who impersonated my father had said. "She sacrificed herself for the Sisterhood of Serpents."

"Elaine was many things, but altruistic was not one of them."

A soup of broth and leeks appeared on the table, brought by unseen servants. Pureed mushrooms swirled in the green soup like modernist dots.

"Frankly, I don't give a fig about altruism. The shadow

demon had my father's memories and he said Lancelot was the Lady's son. Not her lover."

"Cannot two opposing things be true?"

I nearly swallowed my spoon.

"Are you really suggesting..."

"I suggest nothing. I witness and report."

I bit my tongue, not seeing the point in arguing anymore. Neither source seemed overly credible, a shadow demon impersonating my father or the Mother of Monsters. Yet, she was there. A witness. Did she have reason to lie?

Nimue pushed back from her chair and stood to her full height, shimmering as if lightly spritzed with golden flaked water. "What a lovely conversation," she said, making it clear she did not enjoy the conversation at all. "Pull the silks completely closed around your bed at night. They're light-blocking to keep out the twilight. And shut your door."

With that ominous last statement, Nimue swept away, a feather on a current. Dinner was over before it had even begun.

4

I tossed and turned, losing any hope of regaining some of my lost sleep in this beautiful, canopied bed. Instead, I kept turning Nimue's words over in my head, truly shaken.

Romaine had been very blasé about the whole thing. He'd shrugged. "What is a little incest between friends?"

"Incest is between families, you dolt! That's what it means," I'd shouted.

Romaine swallowed his soup, grinning like the demon he was. "Go to bed, Birdie. Let this go. As it turns out, Lancelot spurned her anyway. You are fine."

"I don't feel fine. I feel... out of control. Everything is out of my control right now. Do you understand that feeling? How could you? You're always in complete control. Nothing is out of your grasp. You're a freaking Duke of Hell! And I'm? I'm... I don't even quite know what I am."

"Look, Birdie. I heard whispers that Asmodeus was involved with your ancestors. There. Does that make you feel better? Elaine might not have been in complete control, either. Asmodeus feeds off of lust. The more twisted, the better."

Which was when I'd finally stalked off, carefully locked my door, and flopped onto my bed.

What was this place where up was down and right was wrong? How could I ever go home and look my daughter and friends in the eye after what I knew, not just about my family, but the world? The freaking Outer Planes! I'd once thought the world was too large. I had no idea.

That was, if I got home. I wasn't quite sure how to do that part, yet. Supposedly, I was supposed to ask Nimue for help to find this stag, but we hadn't exactly gotten around to asking her any of the important questions.

I took a deep breath and tried to calm myself. Tomorrow was a new day, or whatever they called it in a place with eternal twilight. I needed to get some sleep and wake up clear headed. Then we could figure out how to charm Nimue. If nothing else we could make a trade. I'm sure we could find something she wanted. Romaine was a Duke of Hell. He had to have a million things he could offer.

My eyes grew heavy and began to close. The soft sound of the waves outside my window lulled me to sleep, pulling me closer and closer to a true night. My limbs grew heavy, my mind finally quiet.

Click.

Instinctively, my head followed the noise. It sounded close. It also sounded like claw on stone. Should I pull back the drapes and look? Would something truly happen, here in my locked room? Nothing had changed from a few hours ago. It was still half-dark and half-light. Forever twilight. Was I less safe now than when I took a bath? The idea seemed preposterous.

Still, my ears did not deceive me. Something crept in my room. I could hear it approaching, a little too quietly, like it was doing its best to remain unheard. I couldn't help myself.

I poked a hole in the drapes and let my eyes adjust. Perhaps, it was a servant, freshening up my linens or a...

Holy, shit! It was a monster.

I could see it in the shadows, its face covered by a curtain of long hair, dripping water from every tangled, black tress. It had a feminine body, curved and sensual, even as it crept along the floor on all fours. As if sensing my awareness, the creature bounded up the canopy of my bed, and for a second, all I could see was her outline and the wet streaks left on the silks by her body. It reminded me of the woman creature, the undine, carved by the alchemist Paracelsus at UFOPP's headquarters. Tria Prima. Salt, sulfur, mercury. I really needed to keep salt on me at all times.

A long rip rent the silks, and the twilight seeped onto my bed covers and across my bare arms. I screamed. Immediately, my protective dome pulsed blue around me. *Tengatur.* The light blue glow of something so warm and familiar nearly blocked out the pain it caused to bring it to life. Nearly. Because it was fear that caused it and fear that fed it. I saw the vivid scar on the neck of the creature bearing down on me. The glowing eyes and that scar were the only things that remained of the elegant woman from dinner.

Nimue.

It had been a murder attempt alright, but a botched beheading seemed more accurate. Medusa-like hair swirled around the immortal monster as she studied me, waiting, seeming to sense that I couldn't hold my protection for long, not when it was born of fear. Through my pain, I considered my options. I could collapse it and try to reform it out of love. I could hold that forever, or at least long enough to get to Romaine, but how? Under the circumstances, did I really think I could find inspiration to reform my protection before she could attack?

A second longer and my bubble faltered. Like a spider sensing a fly caught in its web, Nimue dropped on me from above. I rolled to the side, barely avoiding the creature's piercing claw. My feet tangled in the silks as I frantically scrabbled out bed. I needed to find Romaine. Or a physical weapon. There was an ewer of water on my nightstand, and I threw the vase with all of my might at the creature's head. Then, without looking, I ran to the door.

It was still locked.

It was still freaking locked! How had Nimue gotten in? Also, could I still call her that when she had clearly gone Grendel's Mother on me? The key hole was fiddly, and I couldn't find the iron key that had accompanied it.

Quickly, I whipped around, searching in the dark for the monster. To be safe, I also checked the ceiling above me. Soft clicks seemed to echo off the stone walls.

"*Sagitta*," I intoned, darting arrows at a blur of movement. One hit its mark, slicing Nimue's arm before impaling itself in the wall behind her. It barely phased her. Not even a grunt of pain. "Seriously," I groaned.

With black blood oozing from her bicep, Nimue stalked forward, dripping water from her hair and body. She was a creature of the deep, and her eyes paralyzed me. I whispered *Tengatur*, the most I could do, more a prayer than anything real, as she grabbed me and hoisted me, protective bubble and all, over the windowsill and into the lagoon.

Water snakes lying on the rocks slithered into the lake as we burst through the calm. I landed on the twisted roots of the willow trees along the edges, but I couldn't get a good enough grip through my bubble. I took one last huge inhale as Nimue dragged me to the deep.

We sank fast.

Lake algae and small fish rippled across my body and

still she dove, her sharp nails digging into my protection, dragging it behind her like prey caught in her talons. The deeper we got, the more fearsome and nearly unrecognizable her face became. I fought wildly, trying to get free of her grip, but I was starting to go cross-eyed from holding my breath for so long.

Still thrashing, my body seized, desperate to get air. I opened my mouth, gasping, and—air. Sweet, precious, glorious air. My bubble kept air for me. That was good to know.

I gulped in the oxygen, and although my head still pounded from the lack of it, I concentrated, knowing I couldn't let my protective bubble pop.

Nimue's black eyes glittered in the lake as we descended. I wished I could do two types of magic at once, but I was deathly afraid of letting anything puncture my dome, so I let her continue swimming, her strong shoulders and legs steadily bringing us to the bottom of the lake.

Would I float to the surface if she managed to kill me? Would Romaine find me? Would he understand that, as a human, I would want my body brought home for my family to mourn me?

I mouthed "let go!" but Nimue relentlessly swam. The light above snuffed out, the twilight realm becoming nothing but inky blackness. I feared how deeply we would go. Would the pressure be the same as in the ocean on Earth? Would it burst my bubble? I didn't see anything anymore; even fish no longer lived at this depth.

And then, a small light. An opening. We drew closer, the mouth gaping before us, and she dragged me through a grotto slick with moss and algae. Without thinking or waiting, I let my dome drop and attacked.

AN.BAR šá-kin.

I threw iron chains across the beast, but snakes slithered from cracks in the pumice and curled around my legs. They curled up my nightgown and clung to my bare skin. Their tongues flicked and lashed at my thighs, and I screamed again, the echoes reverberating in the tiny space.

We thrashed on the floor of the grotto, Nimue looking a little shocked that she hadn't beaten me into submission yet. The iron chains twisted around her throat.

"I've faced worse than witches and monsters," I told her, pinching off a snake that had gotten to my waist.

"I don't care about you and your false bravado," she said thickly, her voice swimming in hatred and completely devoid of its earlier grace. "All I want is what is rightfully mine. Give me back Excalibur."

"What?"

"The sword is not for humans or even half-humans. It is mine."

"Great, but I don't have it! I never had it, otherwise I'd be the freaking king of England!"

"Stupid woman, it doesn't bestow kingship. I do that. Your ancestor, Elaine of Shalott, took the sword from Arthur. I care not for the little boy king's pathetic grip on power, but I desire my sword. It is mine by all rights."

My magic felt dampened in this space. I tried to feel for the vibrations of the living creatures, to take their energy for my own, nothing created nor destroyed, but I couldn't. I was stuck in the powerful nexus of her currents, her realm, her rules. There was no escape.

"Correct me if I'm wrong, but I don't think this is how you're supposed to treat guests," I told her.

She hissed in response, and all of the snakes hissed with her. "You are no guest. You are a thief. Give it back!"

"I don't have it!" I yelled, feeling petulant, wet and cold.

The snakes were staring at me like predators, and I still felt the ghostly tracks of their bodies slithering on me. I wanted to do a full-body shiver to dispel the heebie-jeebies they gave me.

Nimue hadn't moved, but I found myself on the ground, her snakes holding me in place like living ropes. I couldn't move, I couldn't breathe. I felt as if I were drowning all over again. Suddenly, a voice echoed around the chamber. Masculine. Familiar. Lovely.

"Oh, hell."

I leaned my head back enough to see Romaine, standing over me, still gorgeous even upside down. "Romaine!" He stood there in white breeches, his shirt half-open, and his horns glistening in the half-night. If he thought I was happy to see him, he was only half right. Sure, I wanted saving, but I had a few things I needed to say first. "You idiot! You told me I'd be safe here."

"I didn't realize she would hold a grudge for so long," he said. "Grudges are a lot of work."

"Feel free to wander. That's what you said."

"And?"

"And I didn't even make it out of my bed before I was attacked."

Nimue watched our conversation in fascination, her eye on Romaine, which was probably the smart thing to do, all things considered. She almost seemed to cower for a moment before the demon, but launched herself at him anyway, as if she couldn't help it, as if she had no choice. I felt the grip of the snakes loosen immediately as her focus shifted.

"Nimue," Romaine roared, his horns lit from their core, pulsing in reds and golds.

Romaine held up a hand and time grew sluggish. I felt

the vibrations of the molecules of Nimue grow colder, slower. Similar to what I'd done to the djinn with Ashavan, Romaine was able to press pause on the monster. He tutted, giving a small shake of his head, his horns bowing down. In mid-lunge, Nimue froze completely, her eyes glittering, but her face a mask of rage. From this angle, her fingernails were long and sharp, ready to draw blood the second Romaine gave way.

"How did you find me?" I gasped, my ears ringing and my body already aching.

"Call it a gut feeling. Also, you two made a terrible amount of noise, and I saw you disappear into the lake."

"Thanks for saving me, I guess, even though you dragged me here in the first place."

"True," Romaine said, as if we had all the time in the world to discuss whether he was more at fault or in line for my gratitude. He rubbed his chin, thoughtfully.

"Romaine, how about we get out of here?" I suggested.

"We still need the stag for our wish. Unless Nimue here knows anything about the stirring shadow magic and Templars?"

Nimue still couldn't move, not even to open her mouth. Romaine waved a finger and her face suddenly sped back up, doing a complicated set of grimaces and scowls before she could talk. Her fingers remained outstretched, one foot hovering off the ground.

"How could I, stuck in this realm as I am?"

Romaine smiled, walking in a circle around her, his bare feet making slapping noises on the wet rock. "Let's not play that game, king-maker. You have your little ways, as do all who have bathed in τὸ ἀθάνατο νερό. The immortal waters."

"That's how you became immortal?" I asked. "You took a bath? Where's this special water at, exactly?"

"Oh, there are other ways and other beings who have found them," Romaine assured me, never taking his eyes off of Nimue. I felt a strange stab in my chest, seeing the way their eyes met. These were beings with such long histories tangled together like webs of silk woven back and forth on shuttles over centuries. I just had to keep telling myself that Romaine was here for me now, and that was what mattered. Or that Romaine didn't matter at all, because he was a freaking Duke of Hell and clearly getting something out of this. Focus! Why was it so hard to focus around this man? Or demon. Or duke. Or whatever.

"What will you do with the stag if you find him?" she asked, signaling some sort of breakdown in her resistance.

"We only seek a bit of his horn."

"And I only seek my sword. Her ancestor cleaved it from my side, and she shall pay the blood price of betrayal!"

"I hardly see how that's fair," I began.

Nimue's eyes turned as hard as coals, as fiery as burning nubs that hadn't gone out for centuries. Even though she was still unable to move anything but her face, a chill coated my skin. I didn't like the look in her eyes.

"Blood price is a tricky thing. I might be able to accept something different. Not so great as Excalibur, but I am the Lady of the Lake. Give me your arm. Let me nick your vein. Let me take a vial."

"My blood?"

I had no intention of letting that happen. Neither did I intend to find Excalibur for her. But I hadn't become a middle aged adept for nothing. I had power within me, waiting to be unleashed.

Before Romaine could say something sensible or try to stop me, I turned up my palms and let the vibrations of the realm, dampened though they were, rage through me. The silk of her dress caught on fire as molecules sped up and her long, wet hair began to steam from the heat.

Nimue let out a scream. Her body contorted as it tried to obey my magic commands while staying locked in Romaine's. I heard cracking as a limb twisted unnaturally and the sudden realization that she was still a living creature hit me. I gasped, releasing all magic, and rubbed my chest. Nimue froze again in that contorted position, no longer having to obey my magic, but still held fast by Romaine's. "Let her down. We're not trying to hurt her."

Romaine tilted his head, watching me curiously.

"That was bad. Was that bad? That was bad, you don't have to tell me. I already know it was." I rubbed my chest where it felt tight and watched the immortal recovering on the ground. "Is she okay?"

Romaine cleared his throat. "Bad? No, little bird. That was good. Very, very good." His horns glowed for a second, and I remembered something that Romaine had said about Blaise. It seemed like ages ago when we were talking about meeting Madame Hortense, the Queen of Shadows, leader of the Divineresses, to pump her for more information. *If the good capitaine is against it, I tend to do the opposite. As a general rule of thumb.*

In other words, if Romaine was encouraging this demonic nature, maybe it wasn't such a great idea. Unlike me, who had at least a little humanity, he had none. I never had to wonder if Blaise had his humanity. In fact, Blaise protected his humanity at all costs. He protected his humanity more than any human I'd ever met, even going so far as to release Naberius, his three-headed raven, from his control against the wishes of his superiors whom he had real respect for. I mean, I didn't have respect for the Cathars, but he did.

The day and night came crashing down, and I began to sink to the rough floor of the grotto. Romaine caught me with one arm before I fell completely. "Birdie," he murmured, "It's almost done. We will find Simon and drop him in the deepest pits of hell."

"Let her go," I said wearily. While I wasn't stupid, I knew, and more importantly, Nimue knew, who had the most power. And it wasn't either of us.

Romaine released the lake monster, and Nimue's face contorted in anger and pain as she nursed her broken wrist.

"You will heal," he told her. "So stop putting on airs for your guests."

"I am old enough to know it is folly to give help in hope of future repayment." She jerked her head at me. "Descendent of Elaine, you should know that better than anyone."

"That is ridiculous—"

"Fine. What will you take?" Romaine interrupted. "Birdie's blood is not an option. Neither is Excalibur. Let me remind you, I hardly need to mention how very *mortal* being immortal can be."

"What does that mean?" I asked.

"The immortality of a mortal is not a guarantee. She will heal, and she will heal quicker than most. She cannot get sick, nor perish from old age. However, most of these things can be taken from her like that." Romaine snapped his fingers. "Of all the ways humans have found to extend their lives, some are better than others. Nimue's way was very good. Good, but not without flaws. The immortal waters have almost disappeared everywhere but here, so her secret is safe, but she cannot ever create more. The water will leave her skin eventually, if she ever dried out completely. Instead, she must stay, alone, if she wishes to survive."

"Those were immortal waters I almost drowned in? Does that mean, I'm—"

"No," they both said in unison.

"Oh," I said, a bit disappointed.

Nimue lifted her chin, still defiant before such a brazen demon as Romaine, and, well, me.

"I will see you at the top," she snarled.

5

In the lambent glow of the twilight hour, we stood beneath the hawthorn trees. Mushrooms glimmered along the edges of the bower, and moss ran in soft tangles up the gnarled trunks. The thorns of the trees looked particularly menacing and sharp.

With the wind chilling the lake water on my skin, I stood shivering, waiting. "Where are these immortal waters?" I asked, a sudden odd feeling suffusing my limbs. Like sitting on a foot too long, pins and needles whiled away at my legs. They felt numb and painful at the same time.

"Not here," Romaine said, half-amused. "Nimue keeps her immortal waters very secure and not even I know where that is."

"You never bothered to ask," she snarled. "Now. My promise? What will you give me in exchange for the whereabouts of the stag? Anything less than Excalibur will simply not do."

"Anything less than Excalibur? Are you kidding? It's a little information. I think the exchange should be a bit more equal, don't you? Words for words, that sort of thing."

"Do you also believe in an eye for an eye?" Her hair lashed back and forth across her back in her agitation. "Because your neck would be my neck, in that case."

"I didn't do that to you!"

"Your ancestor did this by stealing Excalibur from me and replacing it with a shadow sword." She bared her neck, and I physically took a step backward from the violence of the cut.

My voice was hushed and trembling when I spoke again. "I did not do this and I cannot atone for it, but I can at least listen to your story. Tell me exactly how you got that scar."

Romaine's face clearly told me he didn't think it mattered where she got it, that things half-obscured by lakes should stay that way, but I liked information. Also, deep down, I felt it was important to Nimue to be seen. Wasn't that true of all of us, mother of monsters or not?

"Beowulf." She spat out the name as if it still tasted of hemlock on her tongue. "The sword at the bottom of the lake, the sword he used to kill me. It was not what it seemed. It was not Excalibur. The shadow magic used to craft it was profane, and I took the brunt of it."

"So, you want Excalibur because you want it to reverse your curse," I guessed.

"Yes," she hissed. "I gave Excalibur willingly to Arthur, and he abused it. When he died, I took it back into my lake, but not for long. Elaine of Shalott stole it, leaving a shadow version in its place. She tricked me. For centuries I kept shadow Excalibur like it was real, never testing it. Living peacefully. When Beowulf came and slayed my son, I went mad. Of course, I did."

"I'm sorry," I said, barely able to imagine losing a child.

She eyed me, gauging my sincerity and finding it true, she continued. "He followed me here, to my lake. He dove to my grotto, took my sword, and tried to cut off my head. Now, I am cursed to stay the monster he made me for half of my twilight day, every day, because of the bite of a cursed, shadow sword. Here. Alone. Without my son. So now you know the cost. I wonder what you will do with it."

"I'll do it."

Romaine's head twisted sharply around. "Bernadette. Do not get sloppy. Do not make mistakes."

Emotions welled up inside of me. I pictured Amandine and had to blink away tears. Then, I rounded on the demon. "Have you sired any children, Romaine? Belphegor? Whatever you wish to be called?" I waited, practically crossing my arms and tapping my foot as I waited for a response. I got none.

"Have you adopted a child, fostered a child, had anything remotely to do with a child whom you loved?"

He made the slightest scowl.

"I'm going to take your silence as a no. Then you have absolutely no idea what it is like to be a parent. None. I'm sorry if her story doesn't move your cold, hard, possibly non-existent heart, but it moves mine enough to make a deal." Without taking my eyes from Romaine's eyes, I addressed the immortal woman. "Nimue, I accept your bargain."

Romaine barked out a half-growl, already protesting, but I continued speaking over him. "When I have completed my quest, I will find Excalibur and strip this curse from you myself. I do not promise to leave you with Excalibur. Does that suffice?"

Nimue nodded. "The terms are sufficient."

"Do you need me to do anything else to make it official?"

She reached out her hands and the lake began to simmer, then glow. Magic poured from the trees, their roots, their leaves. Frogs began to sing, the fish jumped. Leaves swirled around me, and I could feel the ancient power of her world coalescing around me, testing me, binding to my words. Then all went still.

"Your pledge in this place is sufficient. I accept the rendering of the curse, and we will discuss Excalibur at another time, for another bargain." With that, Nimue bowed her head. Her hair, perennially dripping wet in her monster form, slowly began to shorten. Inch by inch, at first slowly, then more rapidly. What witchcraft was this?

The strands twisted and coiled, then hardened as if some invisible hand slicked them with gel until they mirrored the points on antlers. In an instant, the rest of the Lady of the Lake was replaced by a glowing white deer with golden horns. A magnificent crown encircled the neck of the beast. Tentatively, she held up her front, right hoof, favoring it, the wrist I'd accidentally broken.

Guilt surged through me again. I'd done that, true, but I'd felt remorse. That had to count for something in my human column. And now I understood why she wanted to make sure our bargain would be fair. It was not simply words for words. It would never be. Not when her very body became the one thing we needed. We would need part of her horn, shaven from her antlers, to make our request. A piece of the Lady of the Lake, kingmaker, cursed one, Grendel's Mother. Another small part of her, taken.

"Did you know *she* was the white stag?" I whispered, in shock and a fair bit of awe.

Romaine didn't say a word. I got the feeling he didn't, though, from the way his lips hung open ever so slightly in surprise. "So the white stag is a white hind," he finally murmured. "There were rumors of a princess found in the white stag's trap. She could never remember where she was from, however, and by night, she was always gone."

"Go get the gold filings before she decides to flee. Or tries to impale me on one of those horns," I whispered. "She only has my word."

"Oh, your word is binding enough."

"Even if I died before accomplishing it?"

"I would never let that happen." Romaine gave me a cocky grin, his shirt still wet and sticking to every hard edge of his chest.

I licked my lips. It was hard not to lust over him, this man who was not quite human and definitely bad. He'd gone to the shadow realm to save me and stood there in his preternatural glory, grinning. Which I guess was the point. Demons were supposed to make you fall.

He swaggered to the hind and took her by a horn. For some reason, I winced. It looked so very... erotic. Primal, perhaps, was a better word. She drooped her great neck, still vividly marked by the red scar, which was made even more grotesque against the creamy white skin of her hind form.

She'd survived a hairy man-child trying to behead her just because she dared to mourn the death of her son. If someone killed my child, revenge would be the first and only thing on my mind. A very long, very painful revenge.

I winced again. Was that anger a checkmark for the human column or the demon column? I really needed to consider keeping a spreadsheet if I was going to continue tallying up my demonic qualities.

Romaine turned to me, nothing in his hands to indicate he was going to shave off a few of her gold filings. He grazed the scar with a tip of his finger. "I can see you're torn, little bird. Don't be. Even immortals of lesser means can survive the worst, so do not worry about a little broken wrist. She wants you to feel sympathy, and if she can manipulate your emotions, she wins."

I swallowed hard, nodding. The white hind snorted through her nose and stamped her foot down. Romaine was right. She was strong and a little broken wrist wouldn't stop her. For all we knew, it might already be healed.

Ever masterfully cool, Romaine bent his head and rubbed his horn to hers. My hand flew to my ears as a great rending noise split the air. Red and gold sparks arced in intricate patterns as Romaine sawed. He caught the fiery hot filaments with his bare hands until they filled his palms. All at once, the sawing stopped, although my knees still quaked from the brutal noise and the strangely erotic act of horns crossing.

The magnificent white hind tossed back her head, and when I blinked, Nimue stood hunched again, dripping wet, a snarling half-monster still, her time to become the elegant Lady of the Lake still hours away. "Make your wish, archdemon," she said, almost like a taunt.

Romaine snapped his fingers again, and a fire swirled in his palms, a tornado, a tempest. The gold filings flew into the whirlwind, and he began to murmur some ancient tongue under his breath as he used another finger to swirl the fiery cyclone up higher and higher. An image began to take form, a scene, another world. The outlines of a house shimmered, warm and inviting. It looked nice, I thought.

Yet Romaine's face suddenly distorted in anger, and he collapsed the fire between both palms, black, acrid smoke pouring through his fingers as he whirled on the monster. "That was not what you promised," he raged.

Nimue's face, inhuman and monstrous, twisted into a smile. "You got the wish you wanted."

"No, I received a nightmare."

"So, it wasn't what you expected, but it gives you what you need."

"This is neither what I expected, nor need," Romaine countered.

"Why?" I demanded, my head swiveling between the two, still trying to cool my raging jealousy. "What's wrong? Do you know this realm?"

"Oh yes. I know this realm. I know who lives there, too." Romaine didn't look worried, just annoyed. I wondered what that meant coming from a powerful demon. Should I be worried? Annoyed? I was definitely annoyed that I felt so out of the loop in front of these two. Also, if it was something that could kill me, I'd like to know. To Romaine, scary, demonic killers probably seemed like mosquitoes to an elephant.

"Who?" I asked. "Who lives there?"

"Niccolò Machiavelli," he said. For a moment, he turned to me, a breathless pause on his face. "And my wife."

6

Camelot.
   Era: Unknown.

THEIR BODIES WERE *slick and glossy with sweat. Hair stuck to their cheeks, and their muscles contorted in odd ways. Love-making was not glamorous when oneself wasn't involved. And sometimes even when one was.*

Elaine found her disdain too much to bear. She could have stayed quiet, she could have turned and left, but she chose not to. She chose to stand in the light.

"It appears you've made your choice, Lancelot."

She had to admit, the shrieking was delightful. She stopped her son's ridiculous excuses with her hand.

"You may have her. I'm not so dramatic as to say that if I can't have you, no one will." Her face hardened to slate. "You will not be able to keep both the girl and the reputation. But, of course, you knew that."

He fell, tangled in the silk bed sheets she had procured for him, his legs wrapped about Guinevere's. "Mother, wait."

"I am going to do what needs to be done. You will stay here and finish your ending. Your choice has been made. I cannot save you from history." She threw a look of contempt over her shoulder. "These are your last moments to enjoy each other."

"You are foul," Guinevere swore, her breast slipping out from under the silk sheet as she trembled in rage.

Elaine fixed her steely gaze on the girl. A chit of a girl, really. "Yes, I am. But someone else will judge us in the afterlife and decide which crime is worse. Don't forget, you will stand in judgment, just as I do."

"Mother, she carries your grandchild," Lancelot said quietly. "Can't you accept your new role?"

"As much as you accepted yours." Elaine of Shalott turned to leave, feeling her age, feeling all of the places where her skin sagged and her joints hurt. Her whole body had been given over to this man-child, just for him to cast her aside when she needed him most. "I will do my duty and take the sword to the world of shadows."

A magicked mirror sat heavy against her own breast, hidden from their view. It was the only way she would be able to see into this realm, into this world, ever again. Not that Lancelot knew that. He would probably rejoice if he knew, she thought sourly.

She paused for only a moment, an overwhelming maternal need to protect her son warring with both her anger at his weakness and her pride at his strength. If their plan was to succeed, Arthur would be stymied. His tyranny over Camelot would fade into the background. Lancelot could have helped the Sisterhood without involving Guinevere, but he didn't. He shirked his duty. His reputation was ruined.

Choices had consequences.

Let him have his child. He would never see it grow. Neither would Guinevere, shunted off into a nunnery by Arthur himself.

Only Elaine would watch. Only Elaine would see. At least, she would have that. In a way. In a mirror.

Romaine was already pulling me into another realm, another world. I hardly had time to catch my breath before the searing sensation enveloped me. Twilight faded into blankness, and when I blinked, the new world came into focus. It had a cool, blue light. I took two steps and stumbled, Romaine catching me deftly. I couldn't move, caught in his arms, scared.

"What do you mean your wife?" I asked. I hated to ask it. I hated to feel so off-center and stupid. I knew nothing.

His face was tight, and I noticed for the first time our new clothing. Here, in this place, we were dressed to live in Italy during the Renaissance.

Romaine wore a doublet and thin hose with a surcoat, all dyed a crimson, oxblood red and patterned with damask from Florentine looms. It was laced with silver thread, and his boots flashed silver buckles. His horns, however, had disappeared. I reached up. My nubbins were gone, too, although it felt as if I now wore a Renaissance-era hair net woven with seed pearls.

I took in the rest of my body. My powder blue silk and

taffeta gown puffed up at the sleeves, the neckline plunging and low. Unlike the other gown, this one, sadly, had a corset with golden stays lacing it tight, too tight. My chest moved rapidly, obscenely, up and down as I struggled to get my bearings.

Romaine grimaced, his mouth a single line.

"I need to know," I said, "what am I walking into? And how will this realm help us find Simon?" When he still didn't answer, I grabbed his hands and squeezed. "Romaine," I said softer. "Look at me."

Finally, he glanced down, reflexively drawing me closer.

"It's going to be fine," he assured me. "I have some unfinished business. That's all."

"A secret wife in another realm is what you call 'unfinished business'?" I said, my voice tinged with anger. "Romaine—"

"Rodrigo!" A new prominent voice interrupted us.

With a last look at me, something unreadable, unfathomable in his eyes, Romaine let me go and turned to face the newcomer.

"Niccolò. It's been too long. How nice to see you."

"How nice to see me? I'm surprised," Niccolò Machiavelli replied, pulling a long face. "You were never one for small talk."

"Pleasantries, that's all."

The man had a sharp, pencil mustache and long, curling brown hair that brushed his shoulders. He eyed Romaine and I like we were long-lost friends. It was nearly as unnerving as seeing Nimue crawl up my canopy bed silks.

"I've been waiting for you for five hundred years."

"Has it been that long?" Romaine asked, clearly stalling. It was very un-Romaine-like. He also kept glancing over the man's shoulder as if waiting for the other shoe to drop.

Machiavelli looked as if he'd never had such perverse pleasure. He also looked as if he had no intention of ending Romaine's agony by mentioning the missing elephant in the room.

Silently, I tried to tease out the threads of their relationship. Was it antagonistic? Friendly? Distant after five centuries of waiting? I got annoyed if I had to wait five minutes. What exactly was the most cunning man in sixteenth century Florence waiting for?

"You are sloth personified but I am not fooled for a second that your mind is as lazy or as slow as your reputation."

Romaine gave no warning. A pearl handled sword glinted for a moment before it was at Machiavelli's throat. A drop of scarlet blood drizzled over the silver metal and dropped to the earth. Romaine's voice was low, but we could all hear him. "Tell me I am slow one more time. In fact, say it slowly, so I can be sure."

Machiavelli laughed—at least, he tried as best he could with a sword cutting into his delicate skin. His Adam's apple bobbed against the metal, and he quickly stopped. "Rodrigo, you bring me so much joy. I thought I was going mad, stuck here all of these years. It turns out, I'm still alive! What a wonderful gift you have brought me, old friend."

"Where is my wife?" Romaine asked, irritated. He dropped the sword and put it back into his gold scabbard, but not before he wiped off the trail of blood onto Machiavelli's tunic.

Machiavelli ignored the red smear across his neck and now sleeve. Instead, he threw his hand around Romaine's shoulders. "Come now, old friend. Time enough for stories. I will welcome you into my home. See what I've done with the place."

Smoothly, Romaine disentangled himself, holding out his elbow to me. "Bernadette, stay close. Machiavelli may try to portray boyish charm, but don't be fooled. He survived the Medici court and me. He is no fool."

Machiavelli grinned as he took the lead. "Oh, Rodrigo. I didn't know how much you cared."

Romaine's grip around my arm felt warm and solid. I took some comfort in his touch, demonic or not, and whispered in his ear. "Nimue said the wish gave us what we need. Do you know what that is?"

Romaine's irritation had not washed away yet. His voice was short and clipped. "No."

"What should we do?"

"Remember how you asked if I ever felt out of control?"

"Yes," I said, tentatively.

"Well, now you get to witness what that does to a demon first hand."

* * *

MACHIAVELLI'S HOME WAS... sumptuous. I wasn't sure how else to describe it. Coffered ceilings, stained glass, velvet damask wall hangings. The size wasn't impressive, but every element was perfectly placed. Most importantly, it had a roaring fire and a beautiful bath.

As I imagined myself soaking in its warm embrace, a movement caught my eye. A shark in shallow water. A caffeinated wobble. Whether it let me on purpose or not, I don't know, but this time, I saw the shadow demon pretending to be my father. His familiar brown eyes bore hatred and misery at me.

Then it lunged.

I recoiled, but it stopped short. Again and again it

attacked, never quite touching me. Was I supposed to fight back? Was it missing on purpose? Was this all in my mind? Romaine hadn't moved, hadn't noticed anything, except for my flinching.

"Birdie?" he asked, his voice full of concern.

"I keep seeing something..."

This time, I didn't flinch, didn't move when the shadow lurched at me. Simon was a monster, sending his shadow servants to imitate my father, but I was a monster, too. I reached out to touch the shadow, to hurt it, to make it leave me alone, and it suddenly recoiled and disappeared. I was left gaping at the space where it was.

"What was that?" Romaine asked sharply. "What did you see?"

I rubbed my hands together, my eyes tired and head pounding. "I'm not sure. I think it's Simon, but maybe it's not. Maybe it's trauma and my imagination all stewing together to make me question my sanity."

I said it half-jokingly, but Romaine nodded. "This is a pocket realm within Earth's realm. It is of my creation. Much as you created your safe space of truth-telling and sunshine, I created this for only those I allowed inside. He shouldn't be able to get here. No one but those I allow can enter, not even shadow demons."

I couldn't say a word. I was too deeply shaken.

He continued, "Unlike where Nimue spends her time in perpetual twilight and perpetual grief, this realm operates more or less within the rules as you know them."

"And you control the door?"

"Yes."

"But I..." I shook my head. Maybe it was nothing but a figment. I hadn't done anything to the demon. I hadn't fought it off in anyway. For now, I let it go. There was too much else going on, anyway.

"Why are we dressed like this then?" I asked, swishing the heavy taffeta around my hips.

"I built this realm on the standards of the time. Since only Machiavelli has lived here, it hasn't moved forward, and I didn't find it necessary to come back and update things."

"So there's no WiFi."

"Basically."

"I knew it was too pretty to be true. How will we know when we've found what we're looking for? As pretty as it is, I don't want to be trapped here for eternity. We don't have that time. For all we know, the Templars have completely taken over mainland Europe and are on their way to the rest of the world. If we stop Simon, we cut off the head of the snake."

"Yes, I agree. It was only a theory originally, but now I know that the whole business with the strigoi Geneviève is connected. He was using her to travel to these realms, sniff out magical objects, and send them back to Earth. It's the only explanation for why she kept coming back and bringing that Beast of Gévaudan with her."

"But we've dealt with objects before."

"Not like these. These objects are more potent. The closer they are to their original state, the more power they have. The two of them were sniffing around all of the planes, searching, bringing them together. Both on Earth and wherever Simon is hiding."

"More powerful than the Grail?" I said, picturing that night in the mountains with the pride of lion shifters and a vengeful Le Maire. Thinking of that made my heart hurt for Anouk and Sophie, Clarette and Amandine. I hoped they were hunkered down somewhere safe, and not throwing themselves into battle with the Templars. I knew Sophie wouldn't back down, especially not with her war belt on, influencing her, but hopefully the rest of them could tie her down in a bunker deep under Bordeterre. Or something.

"Much more powerful."

"How do you find my manor?" Machiavelli asked as he came into the room, stilting the rest of our conversation. He held a glass of ruby red wine in each hand.

I took mine and opened my mouth to give a polite compliment, but Romaine interrupted.

"My wife?" he asked, his arms folded and his toe tapping. "Where is she? She never could keep quiet for long, so I must know what you've done with her. Well? What have you done with her?"

"Romaine, calm down," I said.

"Romaine is it now, Rodrigo?" Machiavelli chortled. "How droll. Only had to change a few letters, did you?"

I didn't have to read minds to know that was his way of calling Romaine lazy. Conspiratorially, Machiavelli leaned in close to me. I could smell yeasty bread and cheese on his breath. "Romaine, as you know him, lost a bet. It's why he came to Earth and stayed. You see, men kept ending up in hell and complaining so loudly that eventually the Devil himself became annoyed. He couldn't put up with anymore whining about their miserable lives and how it wasn't their fault they did bad things."

"I'm sure it wasn't," I said dryly, scooting just out of his reach.

A sleek, white cat jumped up on the table. It had orange ears and an orange striped tail, but the rest of it was pure white. With a hiss at Romaine, it went immediately to Machiavelli, nuzzled his cheek, and licked the spot on his neck where the blood had dried and crusted over. He picked her up, cooing over the beast, and gave it an affectionate kiss between its gemstone blue eyes. "This animal is the only thing here that keeps me sane," Machiavelli said, petting the cat between her eyes. "We have been together for what... centuries, my love?"

The cat meowed, chirruped, and gave him a nibble on his ear, all while we stared in undisguised fascination. Machiavelli had quite literally gone insane. The animal had a few intense vibrations suggesting power of some sort, but what that meant, I had no idea.

"Go on now," he murmured. "Your sharpening post is in the other room."

"You mean scratching post?" I asked.

"Yes, of course."

With a parting hiss for the demon and an ambivalent ear flick for me, the cat jumped back to the hearth and left, tail straight up in the air with only a little crook at the top, the tiniest of question marks.

Machiavelli returned to his tale, and I had to admit, I was engrossed by all of it. How Machiavelli had survived here for so long, how Romaine first came to stay on Earth, why our wish sent us here, of all the places in all the realms. I thought Romaine had been the ambassador to France and apparently hung out in Assyria. I never realized he'd done a short stint in Florence, too. Or anything else about him.

"The Devil demanded to know what the hell was going on. You see, every single one of those men said the same thing. Do you know what it was?"

I glanced at Romaine who was sitting with his boots on the table, leaning back in his chair with his arms crossed and a scowl spread across his face. Perfectly coiffed and composed Romaine, scowling like a petulant child. I never thought I'd see the day.

"No. I don't."

Machiavelli's grin widened. "They claimed it was their wives who had made their lives such hell."

I made noises of outrage in my throat. History was filled with stories and poems, art and films, about men who think they were destroyed because of a woman's love when they only needed some self-reflection. No thank you. I'd prefer not to buy into that stereotype, but Machiavelli continued as if he hadn't noticed my annoyance.

"Of course, the Devil thought it funny to send Belphegor, lord of the lazy, but nonetheless, Belphegor arrived."

"Alone?"

"No. He came bearing one hundred thousand ducats, a little something to help him begin his experiment right next to me in Florence. As ordered, I helped him procure a beautiful villa and an even more beautiful wife. Then I put them in all of the right places, in front of all of the right people. Their lives should have been easy." Machiavelli turned to Romaine now, curling one side of his mustache between his fingers as he gazed thoughtfully at the still-scowling demon. "How long did it take before you tried killing her the first time?"

Romaine's scowl deepened, if possible. Machiavelli was really getting under his skin. I think it might have been because he wasn't cowed, not even when Romaine drew blood. The man had lived way past his time, he was just giddy to have company again. Poking the bear, so to speak, was a bonus. Our arrival was the best thing to happen to him in hundreds of years.

Machiavelli waved his hands, four rings glinting in the light. "Ah, it doesn't matter. Onesta, that was the dear woman's name, took him for all he had. Every last ducat and then some. Belphegor was reduced to poverty, driven into debt, hounded by the meanest of collectors. He fled back to Hell, completely denouncing the institution of marriage and women in general."

"Oh did he?" I said, our eyes never leaving each other's faces. Romaine's were cool and unfathomable.

"Oh yes," Machiavelli continued. "Then, I wrote about it for a book."

I broke off eye contact. I couldn't hold it any longer. Not when I understood nothing. "Seriously? You immortalized his marriage? Well that's why he's mad at you."

"I called it, *The Demon Has Met his Match*. Catchy, no? Wait, you've never heard of it? You came from Earth, correct? Don't tell me it's out of print. My publishers promised me a decent sized run."

At that, I couldn't help but snort a little. It was funny. All of it. The name, the whole premise, the idea that Romaine was run off of Earth by a woman. That Machiavelli had no idea how much the world had changed. Every last little bit.

Romaine, however, banged his chair down on all four legs. He stood, loudly demanding to be taken to his wife. "She has something to do with this ridiculous wish. I know it. And yes. Your stupid book is out of print. No one in this century or the last three centuries has heard of it."

"What a shame. I was partial to it. As for Onesta, you've already been introduced."

Romaine hunched his shoulders slightly, giving himself a hunted look. I hadn't even met the woman, and I was mesmerized by her ability to frighten Belphegor, Duke of Hell. Even Nimue was scared of him and she was the mother of monsters, maker of kings!

"We have?" I asked.

A yowl split the air. Romaine and I jumped. Only Machiavelli remained seated, smiling inanely, and I began to understand how he'd survived at so many devious courts—and also how mad he'd gone here by himself for so long.

All at once, the flame-point cat darted from the darkness, latching onto Romaine's shoulders, forcing him to stomp around the room as the cat clawed his tunic to shreds. Never once did the cat stop wailing, but he was joined by a second voice, which I soon realized was Romaine's.

"Are you saying his wife is... are you saying that cat is Onesta?" I asked Machiavelli.

"*Certo.* She's also been waiting for five hundred years to see Rodrig—I mean, Romaine."

"Why exactly is she a cat?" I asked, doing my best to ignore the chaos between the former spouses.

"It was the only way to sneak her with me into this realm. Romaine banished me here for my part in finding Onesta to serve as his bride. For some reason, he considers her a nuisance."

"Weird," I said, watching red welts spread across Romaine's left cheek. "Can he not use his magic on her? He's getting clawed alive."

"He cannot," Machiavelli confirmed happily. "She's wearing a dampening collar. It contained her womanly powers, but it also hid her from his over-arching gaze. Onesta has dreamt of nothing else than marring his perfect face."

"Well, she's doing a good job."

"Yes, she certainly is. You see, he cursed her as he fled, relegating her to lurk in the shadows as the beast he claimed she was, to eat nothing but scraps and have nothing but hatred in her heart. On that count, he failed. Cats are quite loving, if you know what you're doing." Machiavelli grinned. "And I consider myself very knowledgeable indeed."

"Her collar," I murmured, doing my best to ignore his last comment. "Interesting."

Through the clods of flying fur, I squinted for a better look. The collar was simple. A piece of leather punched with a few holes to adjust the size and one silver buckle. No bell or name tag. Nothing special at all to suggest power. Although now I realized the vibrations I'd felt were not emanating from the cat—they were coming from the collar. "Interesting," I repeated to myself, wondering how long I should let Onesta have her revenge on Romaine before I stepped in and separated the two of them. To be honest, Romaine could stand to be taken down a peg or two, and it seemed Onesta was the only woman in the world who had managed to do it so successfully that she'd ended up cursed for eternity.

"So Romaine cursed her, and put this collar on her?"

"Yes, which allowed me to sneak her with me when he banished me."

I kept to myself that Romaine clearly knew she was here all along, but I didn't see the point in mentioning that. "What happens if we take the collar off?"

"I've tried. It's impervious to most things. Although I am not magical, not like a demon, I am resourceful. I have experimented and I have failed many times."

"Hm."

Machiavelli turned hopeful eyes on me, and for the first time since meeting, I sensed his true purpose. He nearly hummed with it. He loved Onesta. They had formed a deep bond, and he now wanted nothing more than to see her free. His devotion was touching. And hell. He hadn't done a thing to deceive or hurt me. I found myself feeling sympathy for the famous Florentine snake.

"Do you think you can release her?" he asked.

"Me alone? No. But I think Romaine can. He crafted the collar, didn't he?"

Machiavelli didn't ball his fists or give any outward signs of anger. He was too polished for that. But he wasn't happy. "He'll never do it if I want it done. He intends to punish me for eternity. That is how demons are. They find your only joy and warp it."

I swallowed a sudden lump in my throat. That was how everyone viewed demons. On an intellectual level, I understood it, but it still didn't feel great to hear it all the time. Yet I was under no illusions that I could change the world's mind about the nature of demons. Or even if I should. If everyone thought so, maybe they had a point.

This was such an exquisite, magnificent sort of torture. Immortality, eternity, alone? Technically, he had the woman he loved with him but only in the form of a cat. It was twisted. It was demonic. It was Romaine to perfection.

"Go for his eyes, my love," Machiavelli suggested.

"Enough!" Romaine bellowed. He was covered in cat scratches and had more than a few puncture wounds. Even as they quickly healed themselves, Onesta delivered more.

The pain must have spurred something deep in Romaine. For the first time since I knew him, he moved with demonic speed, his anger overcoming his sloth nature. His hand grabbed hold of the cat's neck, and he twisted and flung her across the room.

"No!" Machiavelli shouted and sprinted to catch the cat, but he was too late.

Like slow motion, the cat flew through the air and began to convulse. Her skin and fur rippled like disturbed lake water. Red smoke curled over her shocked face.

I turned to stare at Romaine—was he really capable of killing the cat? "I can't believe you..."

"What?" he asked. "Let her go?"

"Huh?"

He dangled the collar from his fingertips, and I whipped my head back. In the cat's place, an elegant woman stood straightening out her dress. Her fiery hair matched the color of the flame-point markings on the cat, although it was completely askew from her tussle with Romaine. Her skin was alabastrine and perfect, like she soaked in lavender-scented milk all night instead of spending the last five hundred years licking her butt with her tongue. Perhaps the exfoliation had helped.

Her eyes were quick, darting. She was still part-predator, albeit a small one. But the moment she laid eyes on Niccolò Machiavelli, the rest of us fell away. She ran to him, curling herself under him, her arms folded at her chest as if she wanted Machiavelli's whole body to simply envelope her, to keep her safe.

I said nothing, but I noticed the tear running down his cheek that splattered on her shoulder. Romaine made a huffing noise, but I elbowed him quiet and beckoned him down the hall.

"That was a nice thing you did," I said.

"Nice? I was just freeing her from my dampening magic so I could be prepared to do something really horrible if I felt the urge."

"Why don't you leave them alone for once?"

"Did you see that witch woman? Did you see what she did?" he insisted, baring both of his arms. I could see hard muscle and the fine hairs on his chest from beneath the shredded tunic, and it was technically blood-splattered, but all of his wounds had already healed.

"You look fine to me."

"That's not the point."

"What is the point, then?"

Romaine sputtered. "I saved you from the shadow realm," he eventually said. "You should be on my side."

"And I am very grateful. Can we go kill Simon now?"

Romaine had a very pouty look on his face, but begrudgingly turned away with me. "Fine. But they didn't tell you all of the story. Onesta deserved no less—"

"Then to spend hundreds of years as a cat while all of her friends and family died without knowing what happened to her? Good job, then. Mission accomplished."

Romaine's perfect face frowned, marring it only slightly. "I don't think you understand the gravity of the situation at the time. And to not even spare a glance, disdainful or not, in my direction after I so kindly removed her collar? Preposterous."

"Let it go, Romaine. If I'd never gotten to say goodbye or see Amandine or Anouk again, scratching up your face would be the least of your worries." I snapped my fingers. "I know. Why don't you explain instead why you are helping me? I've heard enough about your reputation as the personification of sloth to wonder why you came. Enough of this, 'because it feels good' crap. I want the truth."

Romaine's eyes blazed for a moment and I took an involuntary step backwards. "Do you doubt me?"

"I doubt everything," I said, keeping my voice steady. "Don't take it personally."

"I take it very personally, my little bird." His voice had lowered so that I needed to lean closer to hear. His change in tone made my head spin and my heart swim upstream.

"That's not an answer," I whispered.

Romaine's hot gaze made the back of my neck turn warm, and the tiny hairs prickled in primal response. He moved a step closer, and we held each other's gazes for a while.

"I don't like things being too far out of balance," he finally said. "Unbalanced things means more work. Work to put them right. Work that I don't care to do. Do you understand yet?"

I had offended him. I could see it, practically feel it radiating off of him. He kept going, though, before I could offer up any sort of apology.

"Does that satisfy you? Does it make sense why the demon of sloth would not want unbalanced, outcast zealots trying to shift the very balance of the world by throwing more magic at it and changing the very fabric of a realm that has been in place for most of time?"

His anger was a living, dangerous thing, and intellectually, I knew not all of it was directed at me. His tangle with Onesta fueled most of it. So I held back and didn't take the bait, although it stung to hear him say he hadn't done it to help me personally, only to keep the status quo. "I can see that you're upset—"

"Good. Then we're leaving."

"Wait! We don't have anything that we came for."

"Yes, we do," he said, holding up the collar.

"That's why we're here? What is a broken-in collar going to do? What could we possibly do with that?"

"What else?" he asked, derision staining his voice like ink blots. "We're going to domesticate a cat."

8
———

By the look on Romaine's face, we had not landed in the place he had in mind.

"Where are we?" I whispered, his eyes frightening me. He resembled something terrible and vengeful, an electric line of anger radiating off of him.

"We're following a dead trail," he said, running his finger through the air and bringing it back to smell. "Simon tricked us."

"How do you know he's not here?"

"Because I do."

I shivered at the sudden breeze and looked around, only then realizing where we were. Fear shot through my limbs, and I had the sudden urge to both jump and cower on the ground with as much of my body as flat as possible. The sudden cold ran all the way to my toes, as it did anytime I looked over the ledge of a high building or bridge.

We were in the clouds. We were sitting on a mossy covered cliff the size of a sedan car, and all I could see were more clouds and mossy cliff tops. Ice flooded my veins.

You aren't afraid of falling. You're afraid of jumping.

No, I told myself. You're very much afraid of slipping on the moss and falling.

Ever since I'd heard that idea in an undergraduate philosophy course, I'd been even more frightened of heights. If I couldn't even trust myself not to jump, who could I trust?

Searching for comfort, I clung to Romaine's hand. His hair was in a topknot, his horns were still, mercifully, absent, and his body swathed in billowing kimono robe belted at the waist like the living incarnation of a Samurai warrior. Two slightly curved swords were tucked into the wide belt, and his feet were housed in softened leather boots.

"Where are we?" I asked again, my voice sufficiently tremulous for the situation. I was also wearing soft, leather shoes and a flowing, silk kimono decorated with pink cherry blossoms. My hair, too, sat on top of my head in a knot, the breeze ruffling the fine hairs on the back of my neck.

Romaine stopped licking the air, presumably done following Simon's sulfur trail, and looked down at me, finally noticing my hand in his. He squeezed.

"Is my little bird afraid of flying?"

"I'm not a real bird," I snapped. "I'll go splat."

He laughed. "No, you won't. But it doesn't matter. There's no point to being here. Simon is gone, and I think I know where he went. The man is after swords. He is after legends."

The way he said that reminded me for a hot moment of another mention of swords. Ashavan had said something similar. "Five," I whispered. "There are five swords of legend."

Romaine's grip tightened around my hand for a second, barely noticeable, the pressure as soft as the silk of my dress. "Yes. Five. What else do you know?"

"Excalibur. Excalibur is one of them. I... I couldn't... It wouldn't let me touch it."

"And yet you promised Nimue to come back exactly with a sword you cannot find and cannot touch to free her from a curse you understand nothing about?" He let off a string of what I assumed were ancient demonic curses before trying to run a hand through his hair as usually did at home when he was annoyed, only to be stopped by the Japanese topknot. He let his hand drop. "Bernadette, you try my patience."

"It's good for you. Consider it life enrichment."

Romaine made a guttural noise deep in his throat that made me hot and tingly. "Mm. Back to the swords. There are others, but the only one that matters to us right now is one. This is the realm where the Japanese gods resided. He was looking for Cloud-Gatherer."

"What is Cloud-Gatherer?"

"The Heavenly Sword of Gathering Clouds controls the element of Air. It was kept hidden in an eight-headed serpent's tail, but an ancient hero of Japan slew the beast, cut it out, and gave it to a goddess to settle a grievance."

I blinked. "That sounds impossible. And dangerous."

"It is. The swords of legend are unbearable to fight. You could never get close, if the wielder knew what they were doing. A whirlwind, a tornado, a blast of icy air. A strike to gather the power of the clouds and a strike to unleash them. That is all it would take."

I swallowed hard. "And if Simon finds them all? No one could hold five swords at once. Right? I mean, it's physically impossible."

Romaine gave me a sharp look. "You've clearly never met the Indian immortals. But Simon wouldn't need to hold five. He would combine the five and hold their combined power to damage all the realms. He could cut slits between them as easily as a knife through gauze."

"Should we look for the swords or for Simon?" I asked.

Romaine rubbed his cheek thoughtfully, and a flicker caught my eye. A slight disturbance in the shadows of the mossy flowers, a movement or a trick of the eye. I knew better than to wave it off as a figment of my imagination. Sometimes, it felt as if I knew too much.

"Shadow demon," I whispered with a nod.

Romaine didn't move physically but I could feel him on high alert. "Worse than a trick is a trap. Simon knows we escaped the orrery. You said he touched you in Nimue's realm?"

Worse than the feeling of falling or jumping or slipping —or anything to do with heights—was the feeling I got when I pictured the orrery taking my blood and scattering it to the realms. To think I ever underestimated Blaise's junior police detective was a horrible, cosmic joke. That little man now threatened the very existence of my world. "Yes. Well, I wasn't sure. It was there and gone, which I guess is the purpose of a shadow. I thought something grabbed my mouth but then I screamed and it was gone. The same thing happened in your pocket realm."

"As I said, that would be impossible."

"I've come to realize the word impossible is ridiculous."

As if toying with us, I felt a wisp of something vibrate against my shoulder. The moment I turned to face it, the demon touched my other shoulder. I stood still, afraid to move too far and fall, letting the shadow play with me, cringing as my skin rose up in goosebumps. "Romaine, help," I whispered.

But he was just as impotent in his ability to track a

shadow demon, a thing of neither light nor dark, air nor earth.

Still hanging onto his hand, I closed my eyes and felt for the disturbances, the pockets of air that vibrated differently, the smells that were too clean, too much like the air after a lightning strike. The smell of a shadow. There—

I reached out as Romaine yelled for me to stop. But it was far too late for that. I had touched the space between light and dark too many times now. Caution was gone.

9

The scene dissolved, like an Etch-a-Sketch shaken. My legs jerked, my body lurched. It only lasted a moment before my feet sunk into something soft. A shadow flitted across the sand, like a hawk wheeling through the sky, there and then gone.

We were somewhere new. Somewhere hot.

Linen stuck to my chest, the dampness forming a bond. The heat could steal one's breath and never give it back. Wherever we were felt arid and dry, a heat too intense to describe. But that wasn't the first thing I noticed. First, I noticed my skin vibrating. If I pressed a finger to my forearm, I could feel it moving, up and down, my blood practically humming with the intensity of this realm. I felt it slugging through my veins like liquid mercury poured into a crucible. I felt potent here. I felt invincible.

"Romaine—" My voice was staggered, hard to expel.

I looked down and whatever headdress I was wearing nearly made me topple over. It was heavy and, by the feel of it, ornately decorated with jewels and filigreed metal of some type. I scooped it off my head to examine it and met the steely, inlaid ruby eyes of a vulture. Its long wings flared down at either side of my head, and I had no doubt as to the imposing figure I must have made wearing it. Covering my body was a thin, diaphanous white shift dress attached with some sort of metal ring that encircled my throat. Golden sandals protected my feet from the burning sand, and my arms were bare except for a gold band around my left bicep. I had a feeling it matched what was around my neck.

Heat waves rose up from the sands in wavy lines. In the bright and blurry distance, I saw three step pyramids and behind me, a large temple complex built inside a kind of oasis with palm trees and greenery demarcating the edges.

Egypt.

Going from the damp and dreary English woods to the chill of Machiavelli's pocket realm to the cold and cloudy altitude of the Japanese realm to this—a realm that mirrored ancient Egypt—was a shock to the system. Romaine stood beside me, also freshly changed to fit our new environment. He wore a white battle kilt and golden sandals, but his chest and abdomen were bare. His body looked bronzed and oiled, his beautiful hair shaved off in this realm, and dark kohl lines winging from his eyelids. He looked dead sexy. Looking at him made my entire body feel on fire. I couldn't stop shaking. I hadn't felt this way in any other realm; I'd felt maybe even a bit sluggish in the last one. But this? This was as if adrenaline tore through my body, punching holes in my veins and setting my skin on fire.

"My body," I gasped. "I can nearly feel the platelets in my blood moving through my veins."

"Every realm is different in regards to its abilities. Things are hotter here, they vibrate faster. It is potent."

"Where's the collar?" I asked.

Romaine pulled the leather collar from a fold inside his kilt. "Right here. Don't worry. I wouldn't have left it. I'm never going back there again. Those two can have each other."

I nodded and took a chance to look around. "Wow. It's so bright here. That palace complex looks a bit like pictures I've seen of Karnak in Egypt. There's even a river flowing in front of it."

"You mean Karnak looks like this. The realm of the Egyptian gods."

"The Egyptian gods... are immortals? Were they once humans, too?"

"Yes. They also found ways to extend their lives and their hold over humanity, although they have since retreated from Earth to live here fully."

I made motions around my head, a sinking feeling in my stomach. "Weren't most of them animal-headed? Is that real, too?"

"Some."

"Were they shifters or something else?"

"Something else," Romaine said, a bit darkly. "They did not drink of the Grail or eat of the immortal peaches of the East or regularly bathe in τὸ ἀθάνατο νερό, the immortal waters, or anything temporary like that, which would need to be replenished to stay immortal."

"What did they do?"

"Dangerous experiments. Come, Birdie. Immortality is not worth the cost of admission in this world."

"Says the already-immortal one," I muttered.

Romaine took my hand, fairly crunching my finger bones between his. "Did not even your mother, a falling star, know better than to extend her life in unnatural ways? Do not tango with things outside of your realm."

"I would argue all ways of life extension would be unnatural. And, am I not my mother's daughter? I'm already not totally of Earth's realm."

"Argue away. I'm too tired to listen. Now, we must find shelter."

"But we need to find Simon. He's here, right?"

Romaine's horns, back to towering a foot over his head, pulsed gold and red. "No. Shelter first."

"Why? What do I need to be afraid of here? I feel invincible."

Romaine stopped his incessant scanning of the dunes and tilted my chin up to stare into my eyes. "Nothing. So long as we find shelter."

The piercing look made my stomach crumple painfully. "Romaine, you're scaring me. You're a very powerful demon, and if I'm feeling some sort of way here, then you must be more powerful than any so-called god. Why aren't you ready to bust down temple doors and drag Simon out screaming?"

"A very vivid image, Bernadette, but lacking context. Come, I know of a cave."

"Honestly? I've sort of had it with caves after Nimue tried to drown me in one."

But Romaine's footprints were already sinking in the deep sand and disappearing in the wind as he strode ahead. I struggled to catch up in my rather tight linen shift.

Eventually, I gave up and resorted to lifting it above my kneecaps, a look I'm sure would have sent ancient Egyptians into convulsions.

* * *

ROMAINE GOT a fire going with a spoken word, *Ignis*. That seemed useful. I filed it away, mouthing it to myself when he wasn't looking. He stoked the fire with a reed stick he'd found and sharpened against a stone.

"Where do you think the immortals of this realm are?" I asked. "The temple structure?"

"Perhaps a few. They hardly get along, so I doubt they're all together."

"What are they like?" I asked.

"Dangerous. Let's just hope we don't meet them. Simon is here for a reason and that reason relates only tangentially to the Egyptian immortals. Namely, their immortality secrets."

"What is Simon really trying to do? And how many more lives do you think he has? Surely he's got to be on his last one."

"I believe so. Le Maire was, and you saw how desperate he became. Simon needs to find a better way to hang onto life than drinking from the Grail. It has to be drunk from every twenty-eight days on a lunar cycle to keep his immortality past this ninth life. It is no sure thing and much too risky for someone as ambitious and as scared as Simon. He'll want to have power, as well. It's not enough to be immortal—he must be at the apex of immortality."

"So he's regathering the Knights Templar and instituting a coup of UFOPP from another realm of existence."

"A very old realm of existence. One of the first, actually."

"It does feel ancient here, which is saying something."

"Remember all of that speculation you had about the tomb of Pharaoh Tutankhamen?"

"And your meteoric swords," I finished. "Yes. And I also remember how coy you were. You had one, but you put the conversation squarely on Blaise by pointing out how his fit the description of the one stolen from UFOPP. We nearly lost our minds and forgot all about yours."

"Ah yes. I did do that. Although it was Fabien who stole it to give to the Cathars."

"Fabien?" I nearly shouted. "He was your rat? Your man on the inside at UFOPP? He tried to kill me!"

Romaine shrugged, merely poking at the fire he'd lit with a sharpened reed. "Don't look so shocked, Birdie. As I said, I am merely trying to maintain the delicate balance of the world. That requires unsavory characters in my employ. You came out better, in the end. Isn't that what's key here?"

I rubbed both of my temples and pressed the heels of my hands into my eye sockets. It only momentarily relieved the pressure that was building in my head. "Fine," I said, my eyes still closed as I massaged my face. "Fine. Forget about Fabien."

"Well it seems I'll have to, since you killed him."

My eyes popped open. "Really, Romaine?"

At that, he gave me a grin. "I'm not saying banishment isn't good for him every once in a while. Just pointing out that I'll have to find a replacement spy as he suffers in hell for eternity. Anyway, continue. What answers were you working out in that brilliant mind of yours?"

"Don't do that. Don't even think about placating me with compliments."

"Me? I would never."

I waved him silent. "Two meteoric, demon-banishing blades made with star blood... They were clearly forged at the orrery with potent, pure blood from the baby."

"Correct."

"King Tut's tomb also held the ouroboros," I said, still trying to tease out the threads by pulling them apart and looking at them laid before me. "The ouroboros, which Madame Hortense used to help find the secret to immortality for herself. She also found out how to forge the iron mask with meteoric iron."

"To be fair, she found some mortal woman living in the fifth century to do that for her. She's no iron smith."

"That is irrelevant information and stop distracting me," I ordered him. Romaine fell silent with an amused grin on his lips. I turned around, so I wouldn't have to stare at his chiseled face.

"The blade. The ouroboros. Both of them found, for the first time, in King Tut's tomb. Penthesilea began the Sisterhood of the Serpents to avenge the death of her sister Hippolyta from male tyrants like Theseus."

"Don't forget the Lady of Shalott joining the Sisterhood to protect the world against King Arthur," Romaine called from behind me, a tone of pure glee in his voice. "Arthur was a tyrant, too. I mean, Elaine tried to commit incest, but—"

"Cut it out," I ordered. "I feel like this means we're coming close to the origins of the Order of Ancients. It has something to do with Tutankhamen. But I'm not sure it matters. It's more important how Simon will use this information. He wants the oldest, most potent magic he can find, and I think we have to assume he wants to figure out a way to get back to our realm in order to wield it, preferably without using another of his shifter lives. He must want to get to the shadow realm and the orrery. With me tied to it. If you hadn't of saved me, Romaine, he would have succeeded."

I felt a presence behind me. Romaine had gotten up and pressed a finger to my shoulder blade, its skin exposed by this linen dress. "Bernadette," he said low, husky. "Turn around."

Slowly, I did as he told me. When our eyes met, it was

fire. That was how I'd always felt about Romaine. He might not be the actual demon of lust, but he personified it just the same.

His fingers slid down my spine and drew circles along my lower back. The heightened sensations of being in this realm nearly sent me into spasms with a single touch. When he lowered his mouth to mine, I rose to meet him. I molded our bodies together, the thin linen of my shift dress hardly a barrier against his bare, hard muscles. My headdress fell off and clanged to the floor as Romaine dipped me backwards, his hands catching my body and his mouth hungry and hot on mine.

The kiss was just as passionate, just as important as in the fields I had created just for that purpose. For kissing demons. I hated how easily I caved, and how deliriously I wanted more.

And then there was a breeze, a coolness rushing between us. Romaine had backed away, leaving me gasping for breath, unable to speak, angry and confused. My mouth was raw from where he'd ravaged it.

"Why?" I finally asked, bringing my fingers to my lips. "Why even bother if you don't want to actually be with me?"

"I don't know why I did that."

I couldn't tell if that was an opening or not, or if I even wanted it to be an opening after what had happened the last time we kissed. It might have only been a few days, but we'd been to monsters' realms and back, together. He was still by my side. So I went for it. I didn't need a happily ever after with him. I just needed something, I realized. So I said that. "It doesn't have to be forever. It doesn't even have to happen twice. But I want to be with you tonight. This sort of kiss doesn't just happen. It's a gift. At least, to me it is."

"Bernadette," he said. "You don't mean what you say. I'm

not a man to be with once or even twice. I'm not a man at all."

I winced at that. I might not be full woman, but in this moment, I felt like one. A rejected one. All I wanted was to burn for one night in his arms. Possible death in the Outer Planes made it all so much more tempting. But it would feel childish to say it again, or to protest or, worse, to beg. I refused to beg for love. I also refused to apologize for the things that I wanted, even if they didn't want me back.

Softly, he said, "It's not you, Birdie. Don't be offended. I kissed you against my better judgment."

"I didn't know a Duke of Hell was capable of having good judgment," I retorted, my back turned to him now.

"Not many taunt me and get away with it, you know." There was a playful note in his voice, but I resolutely ignored it. I would not be mollified so easily. I didn't even bother turning around, acutely aware of where he was in relation to me. Despite everything, I knew Romaine wouldn't hurt me, and I also knew I'd put up a pretty good fight if it came down to it. "I'm happy to be one of the few."

"There are also very few who refuse to even look at me."

"Happy to expand your horizons."

"Bernadette. Come now."

"No."

"Fine." I heard an odd movement and then nothing. After a few minutes of complete silence, I couldn't help peeking.

The cave was empty. I ran to the mouth and looked around the dunes, but I couldn't even find a footprint. The wind had picked up, rolling sheets of sand across the tops of the dunes. "Romaine?" I called, my voice weak in the wind. Darkness rose up, the entire sky obscured by the incoming sand storm.

"Romaine!" I shouted, cupping my hands over my mouth and closing my eyes against the sting of the sand. I retreated back into the cave, now nearly completely dark except for the still-crackling fire. I picked up the sharpened reed he'd made and held it out. This could be a normal storm—or it might not be. I'd rather have a weapon at the ready. For an hour, I stayed like that, fear clutching at my rib bones, swinging into my heart. When I heard I noise at the mouth of the cave, I didn't think; I only reacted. I flung the stick end over end only for it to be caught by Romaine an inch from his left eye. He examined it carefully before carelessly flinging it into the fire.

"Jumpy, my little bird? Or perhaps you were worried about me after all. I think you do care."

"Romaine, you slimy snake. How dare you stalk off and leave me in some wild plane of existence that I know nothing about. You're the one who rejected me, remember? I should be testing you!"

He was back, silhouetted against the mounting storm, the wind swirling his battle kilt around his tone legs. Of course, he was grinning. "You test my limits every day. Do not worry about that."

I opened and closed my mouth, feeling the grit of the sand all over, the friction of the grains, and the sudden heat bubbling up within my body again. With a last glare, I stalked to the dim back of the cave and settled down to wait out the storm. I couldn't handle any more of his hot and cold behavior. I just wanted to burn with him, and he wouldn't even indulge me in that. He was officially the worst demon of sin I'd ever met. I hoped to never meet any others.

When Romaine came over, I didn't look at him. He spoke anyway.

"Birdie, it's complicated." He waited patiently for me to say something.

Finally, I complied. "You think I don't know that?"

"I think you know a lot, despite only recently being introduced into this world. But it's not enough. I am intrigued by you. Don't ever doubt that."

"Yeah well, I guess it's not enough," I said, parroting his words back to him. "Leave me alone, Romaine. I haven't slept properly in days. I'm irritable. I'm exhausted. Frankly, I'm scared out of my mind. I need to rest."

"You can and you should. I thought perhaps you'd like to see what I was searching for when I went out in the storm."

Quickly, I turned, my eyes settling on a manuscript balancing carefully between his hands.

"It has been transcribed here from the original written on the belly of a thousand newly hatched crocodiles, their skin flayed from their bones." He laid it on a rock on the floor of the cave, but I merely turned back around. Obviously, I was going to read it. I loved knowledge too much. But I wasn't going to act grateful. I was going to set boundaries.

I felt a feather light touch on my shoulder. Romaine had kissed it before going back to tend to the fire as the unnatural sand storm roared just outside the cave. I heard him whisper. "Sleep well, my little bird. In the morning, we have dragons to slay."

I waited until I couldn't feel his presence anymore, and then, hungrily, I began to read.

10

Tablet II of the God of Fifty Names.
Uruk, Sumer.

AT MY TRIUMPH, *at the moment of it all, I had failed. I am the wielder of the fire sword, quick as flame, a sword so old it has no name. I hold the net, the net that resists all touch. I wear the crown, the crown of gods.*

First, I took the immortals of Mesopotamia to council. I used their laws and their fears against them. I had nothing but my words, but my tongue is quicksilver; it is mightier than the sword. Then, I took their power. I took their followers, their weapons, their praise. When they had nothing left to give, I took their names. I am the God of Fifty Names. They are long forgotten.

The beast of chaos, the great mother of the deep, is finally quiet. After I slit her throat, I blew up her lungs to create the sky and poured the Tigris and Euphrates from her eyes. Her breasts became mountains and her spittle the sea. Humankind thanked me, and now I sit in my tower of sand and stone. I can sense I am not alone, for I can feel others prowling. They are looking for ways into my realm. They know what I did, what I can do, and they wish to do the same to me. But the Flaming Sword is mine. It obeys me.

I haven't left my throne for days, gripping the flames between my fingers and watching, watching, waiting. The flames are playing tricks on my mind.

Amon-Ra was first. He didn't merely want to trespass into my realm to menace me; he wished to take it for his own. He watched me unceasingly. He figured out my secret. He figured out how to take others' stories and twist them as his own. I stole fifty names, but he will try to steal me.

I'd heard the rumors, how the great Egyptians slayed a chaos serpent. It hadn't taken long for Amon-Ra to take my slaying of the chaos deep and use it as his own story foundation. Now, he wanted the Flaming Sword as a sort of physical proof that he did what I had done. He wanted this thing of beauty, crafted to carve entire realms into submission. With it, I had made the world from the body of chaos. I had done a good thing. Still today, I maintain my innocence in that.

Now, I was alone as a thanks for my work, and the prowling ones were coming.

The immortal with a body of a crocodile.

The bronzed god with skin too brilliant to look at.

The jackal.

The lion-woman.

The green-skinned god.

They smelled like sulfur from their brush with the arcane. They tried to touch immortality and they paid the price. They came with nothing, expecting everything.

Even a god with a sword and an unbreakable net can be over-whelmed when he is alone and surrounded by his enemies.

I was triumphant. The gods I took to council were all gone. Now, the new ones came for me, and I could not fight them alone.

I write this in my exile without access to my immortality cure. I have done great deeds, and I fear my name will be buried in the sands, a fistful lost to the violent winds of the Egyptians. To pay penance, I write now some of the names who came before me, of those I stole, of their deeds I did not do. Anu. Enlil. Enki. Inana. Ninurta. Namtar. Ninlil. Nirgal. Nanna. Ereshkigal.

And I am Marduk.

Do not forget my name.

11

The temple complex in this realm was double, or perhaps even triple, the size of the human one built on Earth. The two great pylons towered over us mere demons, and the obelisk stood so tall, it scraped the ceiling of the sky and left dark smudges in the atmosphere. Instead of stone, here, they were towering walls of gold, built to intimidate, and they did their job very well. Even Romaine, who was over six feet tall in his human guise, only came up to the middle of the base of the column. The actual column drum sat far out of our reach, and the carved capital, which I knew resembled a lotus flower, perched too high to see.

Although, even in ancient Egypt, temples were not for masses of unwashed, everyday people. They were for mysteries. For pharaohs to commune with their gods. On Earth, all of this was for the glory of the men who called themselves gods. So what were they for here, where there were only gods? I could only guess, but my gut told me something terrible.

Sculptures flanked the entrance. There were images of pharaohs killing men on their knees, crocodile gods snapping men in half, lion-headed goddesses with their faces smeared in gemstone-powdered blood. Everywhere I turned I found death and destruction. I repeated the words of the single-page manuscript, the lost words of the god of fifty names, Marduk. *I write this in my exile without access to my immortality cure. I have done great deeds, and I fear my name will be buried in the sands, a fistful lost to the violent winds of the Egyptians.*

These immortals had usurped and unseated each other through the sands of time, their human nature following them into eternity. That was the saddest bit. That perhaps we couldn't escape our nature, no matter how much we shaped our environment or overcame adversity or even cured death itself. Violence, the need to conquer, always won.

"Ready?" Romaine asked.

I nodded, although the entry hall was even more somber and foreboding, and I actually wanted to say not really. Not at all. I had to keep reminding myself that I was what mere mortals were supposed to fear when they walked through the dark. Demons. Death. Magic.

Me.

Although, on the other hand, I doubted demons during ancient Egypt had to watch how hard they laughed or they'd pee their pants. Hopefully immortality cured that, at least, or else why have it?

The vibrations varied in intensity as we moved through the temple. Some chambers felt merely like places to pass through, while others made me physically flinch if they caught me off-guard.

I let out a painfully held breath as we finally made it through the other side of the dark, exiting the final hypostyle and stepping into the light of the inner courtyard.

Already, the sun beat down mercilessly, hotter than any place on Earth. Palm trees rose up in the middle, providing spots of cooler comfort as their shade dappled the sand beneath our feet. Chambers radiated out in every direction, each with their own feel.

Up ahead and to my left, I felt one with extremely strong vibrations, nearly like a sonic boom that echoed across time. I exchanged a look with Romaine. He shrugged, one eyebrow raised. It felt as if we couldn't speak—shouldn't speak—in this place or in this time. Danger lurked, sleeping, but not gone. Dormant, but not dead. Anything might stir it.

Quietly, we made our way to the chamber where the vibrations were the strongest. Before I even stepped a bejeweled foot inside, it sent shards of ice through my veins. It had residual vibrations that felt infinite and unknowable. Something horrible had happened here.

I couldn't help it; I had to give voice to my fears, to make them not as scary. To be comforted, perhaps. I whispered, "Romaine, I feel... death."

He was looking at the lotus columns that held up the roof of the temple complex. Chiseled into the stone were hieroglyphs, and I thought it was possible they had once been painted. There were still flecks of lapis lazuli blue and carmine red; only the boldest had lasted.

His voice was equally hushed, his fingers tracing the symbols. I came to join him and saw I had been wrong. At the top was a garland of stars. They weren't hieroglyphs at all. This was the language of the meteoric blades. Of the shadow realm script. It was unfathomable. It was infinite.

What the actual hell was it doing here?

"Do you feel it?" Romaine asked quietly.

"You mean something besides death and decay?"

"Yes, something else. This is where the Egyptian gods found immortality."

"Romaine, you said their brand of immortality wasn't worth it. What did you mean?"

He turned his unfathomable eyes on me. "You know what the Egyptians thought of their gods, correct?"

"They thought they were terrifying. Their gods reflected their environment. Much like the desert, the gods were unpredictable. Floods, droughts, storms, anything could happen at any moment—or not at all. Famine and disease were common. They were scary. The world was scary."

"Yes. For good reason. The animal heads you saw weren't metaphors, they were truths. Their immortality cure reflected onto them the very baseness of themselves. Do you know how hard it is to look into your own eyes in the mirror and know who you really are deep down? To know that everyone else could see it too, if they looked at you properly?"

I swallowed. Yes. I had those days. When I was brave enough to look. We all did, I think.

"Well, the Egyptian gods have to see it constantly. A constant reminder of their true, base instincts."

"That's horrible. They must have gone mad after so many millennia like that. Wait, do you mean the animal heads? That's what displays their true nature?"

"Bien sur. The hawk of Horus. The ibis of Thoth. The horns of Hathor. The jackal of Anubis."

"Didn't one have a crocodile head?" I asked uneasily.

"Sobek," Romaine said, before adding darkly, "And it was more than just his head that became the beast."

Under the archway of an alcove in the back room, I saw images drawn and painted into the walls that reminded me of Madame Hortense's lab. Alchemy. It was only a gut feeling, but this was how they'd done it. This was their recipe to achieve immortality. To become gods. There was a stirring in my soul, something that called to me. I could feel the vibrations deep within my chest rippling outwards, like a stone thrown into still waters.

I saw bronzed men and women distilling liquids, melding metals to their structures. There were lotus blossoms as big as a warrior's shield held between their palms.

"That's mercury and gold melted together and suspended in a drinkable liquid state," Romaine explained. "The substance must be consumed from the lotus flower that was grown here under the black moon."

"Sounds complicated."

"As it must be. Nothing less than eternal life is at stake. It is why the lotus is carved into all Egyptian tombs. It represents immortality, because it was the secret to it. But the metals corroded and grew more toxic in their bodies. As I told Nimue, there is no perfect recipe to achieve everlasting life."

"Not even yours?" I asked.

Romaine turned his luminous gold demon eyes on me. "Especially not mine."

The vibrations grew so strong, they shook the foundations of the temple. Dust and debris fell from the ceiling and capitals, and the ground quaked beneath our feet. Romaine's curved horns lit from their core within, and he bent at the waist, crouched and ready to fight. I'd never seen him look so animalistic before. He had a feral energy that was completely at odds with his dapper, relaxed energy. This was ten times worse than his quarrel with Onesta when he was more annoyed and emotionally out of sorts.

"What is that? What is coming?"

He snarled. "Sobek. I can smell his reptilian stench from

here. Prepare yourself. That dome is of little use to me. Take your power and stand beside me."

"Against a crocodile god gone mad? Have you gone mad?"

"I told you we must slay dragons."

"Dragons sound better, actually."

And then I heard it. The slither of a scaled tail. Sobek was coming. The reed torches Romaine had lit as we walked guttered out first. Then I smelled it, too. A deep, earthy scent gone rotten. I saw Romaine's eyes dilate in the darkness. It was silty, like the Nile. When Sobek roared, it battered the temple walls. I threw my hands over my head to protect myself from falling chunks of mortar.

Romaine quickly lit one of the torches that had gone out, *Ignis*, and the shadow of the half-man, half-crocodile illuminated against the stone walls. The god had a hunched back rippling with scales and muscles. His snout was long and his teeth sharp and crooked, each one nearly the length of my forearm, but it was his sparkling eyes, jet black until illuminated by the light, that scared me the most. Over thousands of years, they had lost their humanity until nothing but a terrifying beast remained.

Caught in the light, Sobek launched himself. With a whip of his thick tail, he sprang ten feet into the air above our heads, roared, and attacked with his claws and jaws gnashing. Romaine caught him by the throat and sent him scrambling, but the concussion of air displaced by the god's attack sent me flying backwards. I crashed into a lotus column, my shoulder taking the brunt of the impact, but my head had also snapped back. I couldn't even breathe and then—a gulp of air and a gasp as I realized how hurt I was.

Sobek hadn't even needed to touch me, yet my head

ached and body was bruised. I put a hand to my skull and came away feeling sticky wetness. Damn. Blood. My blood.

As if lured by its scent, by blood in the air, Sobek forgot about the demon in front of him and bore down on me. I didn't have time to think or struggle to my feet. I had to act. Pulling my dome around me, tears of pain and frustration poured down my cheeks. Sobek hit the dome snout first, snapping at it like a deranged animal, which he was, at this point. Threads of power flew from the points where his jagged teeth hit the protective exterior. He roared in frustration, but I held on long enough for Romaine to—

Run away.

For Romaine to turn tail and flee.

12

"Romaine, help!" What the hell was he doing? Surely not running away while I distracted Sobek? Surely not. Yet, there he went.

I was incandescently, majestically wroth. "Get back here!" I screamed, pounding at my own protective dome as Sobek met my fists on the other side, blood and saliva dripping from his maw as he roared again and again. "You coward!"

I felt hot tears of anger at the corners of my eyes, which made me angrier. I wasn't afraid, not right now. I was mad. That lazy, no good coward.

"You can't abandon me!" I shouted, crying again as the unhinged crocodile god lunged for me. I didn't quite understand the visceral reaction I was having to seeing Romaine flee, even if just for a moment, but there it was. Lately, it felt as if everyone was abandoning me. My father, while admittedly a very good copy done by a shadow demon, was only the latest in a recent string of abandonments going back to my husband. Matthew had to go and die. My mother had to go and die. Everyone left me behind.

Anouk's face wavered in front of me, a visual rejoinder from some recessed part of my brain. She would never. She was as dear as a sister to me now. And Sophie. Despite the power of the Hippolyta's belt influencing her, we were still her priority. She pulled herself away from the battle to flee with us, her love for us more powerful than the hatred of the belt. *You aren't truly alone*, my mind seemed to be telling me. *You are never truly alone anymore.*

With a primal scream that would have made a Celtic queen proud, I shattered my own dome. Pieces of it crystallized and became shrapnel, dagger sharp and six inches long. In a defiant display, I threw my hands at Sobek and the daggers obeyed, driving hard through the air directly to the crocodile god.

The shorter pieces didn't pierce through Sobek's tough hide, but at least five of the larger ones went straight through him. Including the one directly into his wide open maw. Before he had time to even roar in response, I screamed again, funneling all of my frustrations and hurt and fear into it. My skin was fire, my nerves exploding in pain along with it. I had no idea what I was doing physically or magically, only that an ancient, feral crocodile immortal was not going to kill me in this place. Not now. Not alone where none of my family would ever find out what happened.

Sobek sank to his knees before face-planting, his body twitching. From his wounds oozed a thick, black blood that was so potent, my eyes immediately watered and my nose burned. His whole self had been corrupted for immortality.

"That was quite something, my little bird."

I whipped around. "Romaine! I will snap those horns off of your stupid head and stab you with them. You like running? Well, you better run. Fast."

Romaine put his hands up to stop my attack, to protect himself against me, because I launched myself at him. But the attack twisted into something soft. I cried and he held me in a tight embrace. I couldn't break free. Or, and this was more likely, I didn't want to. I wanted him to hold me and tell me what he'd done and why.

"I know you weren't running away, Romaine," I whispered, low and hoarse, every inch of my skin on fire from the realm's power and my own rage. "So explain yourself. Go ahead."

"Look, Birdie," he said, pointing out into the dunes from among the columns. "Our presence has punched a hole in Simon's defenses. Any and every god of old is crawling back here as fast as their distorted bodies will let them. They want what's deep inside this temple."

"That's not an answer."

"It is. The only way to find Simon was to figure out where the most unhinged of the gods were prowling. Now we have our answer." He grabbed my arm, yanking me closer, his golden eyes and horns dangerously bright and close to my face. "If you think for a moment that I would have saved you just to abandon you, then go."

"Then why did you?"

"I may want and strive for balance, but I have been around long enough to know I will come out fine on the other side, whatever may happen. I don't need to help you save your realm from Templars and Simon. I do it for you."

I gaped at him, unable to process everything he was saying. My chest was still heaving, and my linen shift dress stretched uncomfortably tight as my lungs tried to take in more oxygen. Romaine felt like he was declaring quite a lot in that statement. But he had literally run away and left me to deal with Sobek on my own. For what? So that he could go look outside and confirm that we were, indeed, in serious trouble? I didn't need to see it to believe it. *Although*, a little voice said, *now you do. Now you're making Romaine show you his loyalty in order to believe him.*

"Say I believe you. What's deep inside this temple?" I asked as Romaine dragged me back inside, past the body of Sobek, deeper into the complex. Sobek's hide was already deflating, like a balloon animal punctured by a needle. If possible, the stink of sulfur and disease, of his body rotting from the inside out, was worse. I didn't think things could physically smell worse than that.

"Another sword of legend."

"Which one?"

"The Flaming Sword is here. What Simon has already done with it is nothing compared to what he can do with all five. Make no mistake, that is what he intends."

"What are we supposed to do about it?"

"Find it. Keep it hidden."

"Maybe we should leave it here under some sand dune. No one will find it."

Romaine gripped my bicep, forcing the gold arm band to cut deep for just a second. "We can discuss what to do with it after we take it from Simon."

"Fine. And just so you know, fine is not a good word in the language of women."

Romaine raised one eyebrow to his perfectly shaved, bronzed and oiled hair line. "Fine back. And just so you know, fine is a perfectly fine word in the language of demons."

"Great."

"Wonderful. Can we continue before the ancient immortals come to eat us?" he asked.

"Lead the way."

Romaine gave a deeply ironic bow and forged ahead, deep inside the twisting tunnels of Karnak. Before long, we came to a room with a ceiling so low that we had to get on our bellies and crawl. The moment we stood, blinking into the light, *Ignis*, I knew it was the Holy of Holies. The walls were filled with jewel toned frescoes that I had never seen in any art history book, but it was the structure at the center that took my breath away. There was a twenty foot pyramid made of crystal with stained etchings along every side. Inside, an obsidian and ivory statue of Amon-Ra towered directly under the capstone. In his hands, he held a curved sword aloft. A khopesh. The ancient Egyptian sword of conquering armies and triumphant pharaohs. But this particular sword was on fire, its flames wavering in through the crystal walls of the pyramid.

"How do we get in?" I asked, desperately feeling all of the smooth corners and finding no latches or creases to indicate a door. My fingernails slid useless on the smooth stone.

"Do you know what the Flaming Sword does?" Romaine asked.

"Of course not."

"It is the sword that created this realm from the chaos monster Tiamat's body. Marduk used it before Amon-Ra stole it from him. It was the sword that forced Adam and Eve from the Garden of Eden."

"What? They were real?"

"That's the part of this story that's tripping you up?"

"Fine. Continue. What does it do?"

"You won't even see it attacking. It slices quicker than the eye, like a flickering flame. Just like real flames leave some things hidden in shadow, the Flaming Sword is able to hide its attack."

I felt a longing deep beneath my ribs. It yearned for the sword. I was no longer Birdie from the Bayou. I was something else entirely. But I could feel more things coming. Looking. Wanting what was mine.

"The Egyptian gods have felt these rumblings. They're all going to descend on this place to feed on us. They haven't fed in a very long time, Birdie. We must find Simon and take his stockpile from him now."

"Take a stockpile of magical weapons from a lion shifter with nothing to lose?" I asked, calmly, even though I wanted to screech. Despite all I'd learned, I was still mortal. Weapons, magical or not, still hurt. Death could still come for me, just as it had my mother. So, I kept my eyes focused on the prize. That sword was mine. And the sooner I claimed it, the sooner we could get out of here.

"Cover me," I ordered Romaine. I closed my eyes, trusting in this inhumane creature to protect me. It was all I could do, really. What other choices were there?

I let my fingernails slide across the smooth gemstone and searched throughout my body and bones for abnormal vibrations. There. Nearly imperceptible was a thin line, a hinge. A doorway in. Our salvation or our doom.

"Hurry, Bernadette," Romaine said, his voice low. "The immortals are coming. Can you smell them?"

"I'm trying not to," I muttered. I let my hand hover over the crack and focused my attention on it. If vibrations were frequencies of matter, and I had manipulated them in various ways before, it stood to reason I could do so again. I could slow them down and slip through the spaces between them, couldn't I?

I felt the tug and pull of the molecules almost as if they were fighting me, not liking the way I manipulated them. It wasn't as if they were sentient; I didn't feel that. Just that I was forcing them to do something against the natural order, contrary to how they had arranged themselves. It wasn't like water, easily diverted when a dam was erected. Or maybe it was exactly like water—any large river of molecules just needed enough force to change its direction. I pushed against the molecules, slowing their vibrations down, pausing the spaces long enough for me to slip past. I became the earthquake strong enough to change the course of rivers.

Like sliding through a slime-coated door, I squeezed my body through and blinked my eyes open. I was inside!

I was inside, but Romaine was not. He banged a fist against the edge of the crystal pyramid, yelling something at me. The sword. I had to get it.

With tunnel vision, I homed in on the statue of Amon-Ra. The khopesh's fire held no heat, but it was still too bright to look at for long. Those strange swirls I'd seen twice before on Romaine and Blaise's daggers, the Widmanstätten patterns, danced up and down the khopesh. Forged in fire and the power of falling meteors, this weapon radiated intense vibrations. There was no doubt it was authentic.

"My apologies, Amon-Ra," I muttered as I placed my foot on the statue of the ancient immortal's kneecap and began to climb up his loincloth. His hand holding the uplifted sword was at least ten feet off the ground, and the metal gave my slick sandals no good purchase. I slipped once, hanging onto the battle kilt with my fingers until I could get my leg high enough to sit for a second and catch my breath in the crook of his bronze arm. It was mostly from adrenaline and fear, rather than any real exertion.

This was the most holy place for ancient Egyptians, and this sword literally created worlds. Maybe I should feel awe, but I only felt excitement. What would I be able to do with it? Vaguely, I remembered I was supposed to be hiding it so bad guy zealots couldn't remake the world in their image and start a second Inquisition, but Romaine could be on to something. Perhaps it was better off with us. With me.

A noise echoed in chamber as my ragged breathing evened out.

I didn't hear the newcomer. I only heard his voice.

"I thought all birds could fly. Shall we see?"

And just like that, I was falling, slipping off the metal, screaming into the abyss. I flailed with all of my limbs, wincing already at the inevitable impact, my spine cracking against the ground, but it didn't come.

I opened my eyes to find myself lying down in swirling mist. There was nothing here. Nothing, except for a movement in the shadows. It felt like a tomb, stuffy and hot, with a vague sense of the morbid.

The world had quite literally tilted, and I went down hard on my knees, my stomach heaving, once, twice. I wiped my mouth and groaned. Only bile came up, hot and sharp in my throat.

Simon.

I scrambled to my feet, cursing under my breath. Where was the khopesh? There, out of the shadows and swirling mist of his own making, was the man from my nightmares. He was taller than I remembered. Still boyish-looking, except for the sneer that twisted his features into something menacing. His eyes could hide nothing; they were the windows into his corrupted soul.

"How frangible you are here," he commented. "How easily breakable. Much like hollow birds' bones."

I couldn't see Romaine or the Holy of Holies anymore. "Where did you take me?"

A laugh, high and cold. This wasn't some junior agent

on the job, trailing after Blaise like a puppy dog. This was a master manipulator who had lived nine lives of abuse, manipulation, and hate. This was the true Simon, stripped of all his illusions and disguises; and yet... I could see in his eyes that his true self was the same cowardly man who let others take the fall or stayed behind his large army of knights while they attacked walled cities and went into the line of arrow fire without him.

"Where are we?" I repeated, killing some time so I could get my bearing and stop my stomach from threatening me so insistently.

"We're in a pocket realm of my creation. Don't worry, your demon lover can't get in, although it wasn't as if he was following you into danger very eagerly. At any rate, we wouldn't want him dancing with my demon. Would we?"

"I only want one thing. To kill you," I snarled, hate flooding me as coldly as the adrenaline, and then I paused. When did I become so bloodthirsty? Was that the demon-influence? Could I take Simon's life? His last life, that was. His ninth, I reminded myself. I remembered sitting at Anouk's kitchen table in Bordeterre reading about how this man had led a crusade against his fellow Frenchmen, butchering mothers and children, all for a play for power. For money. For land. For prestige. These things were more important than innocent human lives. But in a beautiful twist of fate, those very women he had been trying to subjugate killed him first with the help of a catapult.

I steadied my shoulders. Yes, I believe I could join that robust, Southern French tradition of women killing wannabe conquerors.

Before I moved to do so, however, I paused. I'd felt something odd, sniffed that tell-tale whiff of sulfur, cleansed by ozone. Then, a shadow flickered out of the corner of my eye.

It had my father's face. I kept my focus on the shadow letting Simon stay in the corners of my periphery.

"So it has been you all along. You've been sending your pet shadow demon to haunt me."

The real Simon shrugged. "Of course."

"Not 'of course'. After your little stunt with the orrery, I barely know what's real anymore."

"All of this is very real and a very good learning exercise for you. It's good for you to know that I can touch you anywhere, and it's good for me to know what your actual weaknesses are. Win-win."

"Yeah, it doesn't sound like a win for anyone."

"Even I must admit, I was impressed watching you during your bout with Nimue. She's quite the old lake hag these days." As he said this, he casually took out a net. The only reason why I recognized it was from reading the tablets given to me by Romaine. The unbreakable net of the God of Fifty Names. Marduk. I'd read some of his words. He'd been forgotten, lost, and exiled, left to die, and maybe that was what he deserved, although I was in no position to judge. He was long gone, but not his net. Was it empty, or was it crammed full of magical objects, as I was beginning to suspect? It was unbreakable and impossible to see inside, but it couldn't hide powerful vibrations and that thing was controlling a small earthquake.

"The Templars are already back in our realm," I said, praying Romaine was still trying to find a way inside. Back-up would be lovely. "Don't you think they've already got a leader and a plan?"

"Of course. And your point?"

"If you show that them they don't need you, then it becomes obvious when you come back, riding in on some demented white horse to save the day, that THEY DON'T NEED YOU. Suddenly, you're superfluous."

"Shut up, infidel. You don't understand the inner workings of the Order or the Templars, and I don't expect you to."

The shadow's face flickered again. It went from my father into a bronze-skinned, teenage boy I had never seen before—I was completely captivated, caught off guard, distracted. I turned my attention for a second from Simon to the shadow demon, wondering who he was supposed to be portraying now.

In that instant, Simon's hands were around my throat as if he wished for nothing more than to kill me the old fashioned way. Strangling was a very visceral, physical thing.

Without pausing to think, I called for my iron bars, feeling the rapidity of this realm's heat and its intensity on my powers over all matter. My pulse quickened to match it.

AN.BAR šá-kin.

Simon took an iron chain to his face, red welts already appearing the shape of the links. His pet shadow evaded everything, however. Neither me nor my chains had been anywhere near quick enough. The shadow demon tossed me off my feet as easily as a flower petal in the wind while Simon struggled on the ground to get free. As I fell, I saw his fingers reaching for his unbreakable net and the powers inside. Horror filled me, knowing something terrible was inside if Simon was schlepping it around.

And then, he pulled out... a vase.

Except, this one was shaped more like an urn—one specifically used for organs during mummification. By the hieroglyphs, I guessed a canopic jar used in ancient Egyptian death rituals.

I was proud of myself for recognizing it. I never would've been able to do that six months ago.

"Vessels to hold the heart but leave the soul. Shall I have Tut rip out your soul?"

Next from the net came a long, bronze instrument that had a hooked end, meant to scramble brains and yank them through nostrils. Of course, the person was usually dead by that point, but I was most decidedly not. Not yet, at least. It vaguely registered that he'd named the shadow Tut. As in the boy pharaoh? But I didn't have time to ponder it. I had barely scrambled back to my feet, my body broken and bruised from the fall, when my feet left the ground and I was soaring through the air, vortexed inside of something small and foul smelling.

I coughed and held my inner elbow up over my nose, but the stench was strong and it was so very dark inside. I was afraid to use *Ignis* without knowing where I was and what I might accidentally set on fire. Then came a voice, muffled and large-sounding.

Simon. Why did it sound so out-of-proportion large? It was a gut-wrenching moment when I figured it out. I was inside the canopic jar.

I banged my fists against the glazed pottery, hearing my voice muffled, too, all bottled up. I felt like a djinn in a bottle, a rat in a trap. I felt fear. Impossibly, he'd put me in the canopic jar for hearts and livers and other squishy things that should stay on the inside of your body.

"Let me out!" I screamed.

"You escaped the orrery and your destiny once, but that's the thing about destiny. It has a way of catching up to you."

I threw all I had into breaking out of that jar, or cracking it at the very least, literally banging my hands against it as I tried to muscle my way out magically. The backbite of magic concussed the air, popping my eardrums.

I felt fear, but there was something else.

I felt the power of the shadow demon drifting outside the jar, its vibrations of another scale to those in my own world, those things I was intimately familiar with. It was a scale built for passing through walls and jumping to new realms.

Slowly, I measured them, mastering their feel and rhythm. I didn't ask; I demanded. I yanked the essence of the shadow into my own shadow, merged it with mine, sucked its power for my own. In an instant, my body flickered. I was there and not there, as fleeting as a shadow in the face of the oncoming dawn. My nose flooded with incense and the fragrance of lotus flowers barely covered the stench of unwashed humans. *Bow before the god incarnate, the living image of Amon-Ra!*

Power flooded my veins. The canopic jar no longer stood in my way. I passed through it the way dark passes through a tunnel, coming out into brilliant white on the other side.

When I looked up, I met Simon's eyes; I enjoyed what I saw.

He wore panic like second nature.

I turned my hands over before the agony started. The shadow had begun to fight back, struggling to escape my orbit. The creature had been as shocked as all of us, but now it was scared as I continued sucking energy from him. It felt like holding the reins of a giant and telling it where to go. I was losing my grip as quickly as I had begun, but I was also getting stronger in proportion to my consumption. This was why the demon was afraid to touch me. Maybe this was even why Ashavan had been afraid to let the shadow touch him. Shadows were the conduit, beings in between light and dark. They were the ones always in control, sucking strength from others for themselves. When I had done the reverse to him in Nimue's realm, he'd felt me trying to sap his strength, and it terrified him. That was what had allowed me to scream—I had broken free by taking back some of his power. The seductive nature of the power of the shadow yanked at me, and I took more and more for my own.

I launched myself at Simon, my entire body prickling with the strength of the shadow. With a quick uppercut, I got in two good hits, blood flying from Simon's mouth. He'd doubled over when I smashed him on the back, and I thought for a moment he was right. Physical violence was visceral, I could see why he wanted to strangle me with his bare hands. I wanted to strangle him with mine.

"Release him," Simon demanded, but to my enhanced ears, it sounded like a squeak. Simon was a squeak. Simon was an insignificant mouse. I wondered what I could do to him with shadow magic at my disposal. I could be the lion playing with the mouse.

And then, for just a second, I thought of my friend. I thought of Clarette, a mouse shifter. She wasn't insignificant. She was magnificent.

I hesitated too long.

Simon used some type of pocket dagger, slashing at the sliver of space between me and the shadow. I fell to my knees, crying out at the pain, gripping my side with both hands as if I expected to see a huge gash and blood pouring from my fingers.

There was nothing; only I could sense the slight shift in vibration of my matter.

"Do you even know who this is?" Simon towered over me, a meteoric dagger clenched in his whitening fist. "You dare fuse a mighty pharaoh to your pathetic body?"

My eyes darted to where the shadow hovered, weaker but still formidable. If it was in half the pain I was in, I would be thankful. There, I was demonic and I liked it.

All around us, I saw the edges of the pocket realm become ragged, like frayed rope. Beneath the translucent edges, the crystal pyramid appeared again. I saw Romaine, slightly fuzzy and out of focus, but still there, waiting for me. Fending off immortal psychopaths. The pocket realm was collapsing, either from the power within in going haywire or the lack of ability on Simon's part to keep it stable. Either way, I just had to force it the rest of the way open. Kind of like cracking an egg.

Simon was still scathing. "This is the mighty Tutankhamen, restorer of his people's religion, founder of the Order of the Ancients, ruler of this realm—"

"Speaker of bullshit, yeah, I get the picture." Inside, however, I was reeling. The thing that killed Ashavan, the thing that had followed me, was the one and only King Tut? Of course. And he'd created the Order of the Ancients? Obviously.

"Tutankhamen was a great ruler who righted the wrongs of his father and fought against the tyranny of his stepmother." While Simon spoke, the shadow, apparently the Pharaoh Tutankhamen, began to slink around behind him. As if I wouldn't notice.

Well, now I was completely attuned to his weird vibrational content. I knew exactly where to look in the shadows to find him. I yanked again. I didn't force him to merge with me. Not entirely. I didn't need that kind of power to accomplish my goal. I simply borrowed a hand—and part of a clubfoot.

My own shadow swallowed them, their addition making me strong. Invincible, even. With a wet snap, the rest of the pocket realm dropped away, plopping us right back in the Holy of Holies.

With that bit of magic accomplished, I let go of Tut immediately and felt his vibrations scamper elsewhere, far, far away from me. Still, everything was blurry, and it took me a moment to regain focus.

Romaine was fighting the Egyptian gods five to one, wielding the sword of flames himself. It kept them at bay but a few gods had managed to get within striking distance on his unprotected sides.

Romaine had taken a spear to his shoulder blade, but it didn't seem to bother him. With a casual glance over his back and an eye roll, he pulled it free with a disgusting squelch and aimed the bloody tip for the immortal with a hawk head. Horus. The god flapped his arms like he forgot he was in a mostly-human shape and squawked as Romaine easily pinned his body to the wall. In an artistic touch, he'd managed to stick him to a part of the wall with frescoed images of Horus himself in better days, accepting tributes and gifts, wings on his back.

"Birdie! I was genuinely worried. Can you believe that?" he asked. A woman in a black linen dress with the head of a black cat flung herself out of nowhere onto my back. Her claws sunk into my skin with red hot agony. "I thought, well, isn't that just it? She's gone and gotten herself killed. I was amazed at the depths of my emotions."

"I'm pretty sure you should still be worried," I yelled, finally getting to use my shiny new word and light the cat goddess Bastet on fire.

Ignis.

In this potent realm, I could do anything. I could reach my full potential. Whatever it was, I could find it here. Bastet yowled, her green eyes luminous and unhinged.

Nothing good had come from immortality for these creatures. Capricious and alone, millennia had corroded them. Their sense of morality, their powers. All weakened. They lived in gray. They lived a life in-between living and dead. It looked like hell.

Romaine could handle the immortals, I decided. He seemed to be immune to them at any rate. I needed to chase down Simon, to stop this madness and set things right before it was too late.

Despite the chaos encircling me, I followed his vibrations and that of his pet shadow demon. Tut. Here in this world, they were too strong to hide and all too easy to track. "Come here, kitty cat," I taunted, wondering if he'd change into a lion, even if it meant he couldn't carry the net of magical goodies. Maybe he'd hold it in his mouth as he ran on all fours. I might pay to see that.

They hadn't gotten far. I caught up to them in the next chamber, lurking in the shadows. Tut trembled at the sound of my approach. I could feel the fear pulsing off his vibrations. I had to admit, I reveled a bit in it. Finally, I wasn't the weak, unknowing one. I wasn't hopeless. All in an instant, Tut was gone. Popped out of this realm and into some other place, perhaps the shadow realm. We wouldn't ever know. Simon must have felt his crony leave at the same moment I had. His face drained of all color and suddenly, I was the bird playing with the lion.

"What else do you have in that net?" I asked casually.

Simon's eyes couldn't hide his truth. He could sense the end. That made him desperate and dangerous. With a knot-tying maneuver, he threw the net into the air. I blinked and it was gone.

"What did you do?" I asked, terrified of the answer. "Where did you send the net?"

"I am simply helping those in need. It is a core tenant of my faith. Vows of obedience, chastity, poverty, these see me through."

"Your faith has been warped," I countered. "There's nothing self-sacrificing about it or you. Not anymore. By my count, you've broken every single one of those vows." Despite my words of bravado, I really didn't like the idea of that net falling to some other plane of existence. What if it landed on Earth? That was exactly the kind of thing Simon would do. Was someone there to receive it or were the magical objects inside merely hurtling to unknown destinations? Either way, it was bad news.

Romaine skidded around the corner. "Birdie, catch!" The collar flew like a frisbee, and I had to jump to reach it, snagging it with my fingertips.

At the same time, Simon shifted into a lion, shaking out his golden mane as he charged. His growl shook the inhuman-sized lotus columns and made earthquakes reverberate around the region. Here in this realm, we were all supercharged. He leapt straight at my face, claws extended, curved and deadly sharp. This time, I promised to make sure the bird caught the cat.

"Watch this bird fly," I said, throwing his words back in his face.

Just as he reached me, I leapt into the air and clamped the collar tightly around Simon's neck, the magical object dampening any interference, spells, or tricks he might have had up his sleeve. The lion mewed.

By the time I landed, Simon had shifted back, whether by the force of the collar or on his own, desperate to use his voice and beg us to remove his new cage, I didn't know. A little kitty bell tinkled against his human neck, and Simon turned purple with rage. A vein over his left eye bulged, and he began to spit profanities, speckles of blood still flying from his mouth where I'd punched him. Patiently, I ignored him and turned to Romaine.

"What are we going to do now?" I asked. "Does UFOPP have a magical prison or judicial system? Not that I'm saying I buy into everything they sell, but if there was some sort of centralized judiciary committee, that might be nice—wait. What are you doing?"

"Immortality does not mean invincibility."

I hadn't seen him move, but Romaine was right next to Simon. He picked him up by the collar, twisting to make Simon's face turn a deeper shade of puce. Romaine's curved demon horns glowed, his face a furious snarl, a pulse of pure evil vibrating through his body as he snapped Simon's neck in half. "It never has."

In an instant, Simon was gone. Romaine let the body fall to the ground, simultaneously ripping the collar off of the dead man's crooked neck and letting it dangle between his fingers. The body was a heap on the ground, odd angles and unfinished edges.

I screamed, completely caught off-guard. Without a second thought, Romaine had killed a helpless Simon, and now he stood there, his face unlined and untroubled. He'd even wiped his fingers on the dead shifter's clothing, as if wiping off muck or something dirty. My hand was still stretched out uselessly to what? Try to stop him? I had never felt so impotent in all of my life, except perhaps, at the death of my husband. Was that what death was? A total loss of control, a complete feeling of emasculation as a human being? Irrationally, I wished Simon had stayed in his lion form, and I hated to admit how much worse it was to watch a human, rather than an animal, slain in front of my eyes.

Madame Hortense's words came back to haunt me. *"You*

are in the crucible now, Bernadette Oriane. You will be revealed for all to see, for better or for worse."

What was I? Better? Or worse? Who was good enough to judge?

Because for just a moment before the horror, I had felt something else. Glee. A balloon of joy had inflated inside of me. That was Simon's last life. I would never have to worry about him menacing me or my family again. I was no better than Romaine and in no place to judge him, cold-hearted as it sounded.

Demonic or all too human—I would never know which side of me dominated my brain more. I would never know who I truly was. I would never fully trust myself again.

Or perhaps the solution was all too simple. I would never wonder again how much of my demon side was influencing me. The answer was obvious.

13

Nefertiti, Queen of Egypt
  Luxor, Egypt. 1323 BCE.

FOR SEVEN YEARS, *Egypt had to learn to live without the most beautiful woman in the world when Nefertiti died. Their people mourned and tried to remember what it was like to live near such bewitching beauty, to have walked as close to perfection as possible. Denied their precious queen, they survived as best they could.*

Except, Nefertiti wasn't dead. She died when her heretic husband died, but unlike him, she was reborn as a pharaoh, rising up from the ashes of his failures. Her death was easily faked, hidden by those loyal to her, above all, by her six beloved daughters. At all costs, the boy Tutankhamen could not be allowed to simply take the throne of Egypt. He was not worthy. He was not of Nefertiti's own blood. A stepson was so useless when her daughters were virile and strong, like her. What was the point of that boy?

Honestly? What was the point?

At first, she thought marrying him to one of her daughters would be enough to control the sickly child. She would keep him a puppet for the optics of a male on the throne. But lately, he had proven difficult, surly, even... disobedient. He kept other wives, although how he pleasured them was beyond her comprehension. He also spent hours in Karnak, away from Luxor, which didn't suit at all. Whispers of rumors still told the stories of the cure for immortality buried deep in the sands there, a mirror of a realm of the dead from where their own gods had descended.

Then, she met a woman who claimed to make pharaohs of women. The stranger claimed to have created Hatshepsut and claimed she could do it again, better this time.

"Better?" Nefertiti had scoffed, her swan neck even longer and more elegant than this foreigner's. "No one remembers these old queens' names. Anyone else would be better. Why, the moment Hatshepsut died, the next pharaoh struck her name and face from every monument he could."

The light-skinned woman with ancient eyes sneered. "Your gods roam the realms, sowing and harvesting havoc among others. Your stepson, while you've kept him at bay, plots against you. Worse, what he does plots against me."

"And who are you?" Nefertiti challenged, used to being hard, to being granite, to being the statue they made of her.

"Immortal, which is all that matters to you. Take the belt I offer. Go to war."

Of course Nefertiti did. She wasn't one to give up power, not even when people died. She still lived, obviously. That was power.

"When will I be immortal?" she asked the foreigner, over and over again.

"When Tut is dead and all of his sparks of discontent are snuffed out. They are leading to fires everywhere."

There was only one thing to do. Kill Tut. Unexpectedly. Quickly. Preferably horribly.

The festival lasted for three days and nights. Clouds of

incense and bursts of cinnamon radiated the air, servants led gold-shod elephants down the streets laden with wine and food to be distributed to the people. For hours at a time, the hot sun was blocked by blizzards of doves, released from wicker baskets all at once. In the middle of the street stood a hollow statue of lightly hammered gold depicting the god of wine and blood, Shezmu, holding aloft a goblet from which wine, thick and sweet, swelled in a waterfall to the crowd below.

And so the people were distracted. And Nefertiti could slip away.

She found her stepson ripping apart a crocodile amongst decaying remains of many animals littering the inner sanctum of a temple where no mortal man was supposed to step foot. Congealed blood lay in shallow pools besides bronze instruments she couldn't begin to name or place their function. It seemed monstrous. He seemed monstrous. He was monstrous and she would be the one to slay him.

The golden belt of war sparkled on her hips, and each arm was covered with bands of gold and lapis lazuli. Her tomb stood empty, waiting for him to occupy it. The whole affair was nearly poetic. So caught up in his unearthly experiments, he hadn't even heard her come in, although he wouldn't have been able to stand and greet her properly anyway. Usually, he had sycophants to do that, but so afraid of them stealing his secret, he had dismissed every last one. The fear in his eyes when he saw they were alone in his secret place was enough to make the blood in her veins sing in anticipation. It was almost a shame to kill him and end her pleasure so soon.

Tutankhamen started when she threw a pebble near his twisted foot. She smiled wide, feeling as luxe and slink as a cat stretching in the sunlight. Then, she made him a promise.

"I will put you in the tomb meant for me and your afterlife

will be nothing but a sham, half a woman, half a man, never whole, just as you are now."

He pulled a thick dagger from his kilt. It glimmered unnaturally in the guttering light of the reed torches, swirls seeming to move on their own accord up and down the metal blade. The incense was thick enough to gag on.

Nefertiti's eyes widened when she saw the blade. "Blasphemy," she whispered. "Just like your heretical father."

"He was your beloved husband," Tut reminded her.

She ignored that. "Do you really believe the gods will call on you if you succeed here? That they would want to take a crippled boy into their bosom? What makes you think they won't be furious that some mortal tried to do what they did?"

"They will take me. I know their secrets and they will have no choice."

Ah, she confirmed in her mind, only guessing before. We both search for the same thing. We both yearn for it.

"What is that weapon? Why does it have those swirls?" she asked.

"I may not be able to walk or run like a man, but the blood of stars will fly for me." He flung the dagger, end over end, directly at her heart. It should have struck deeply without any hope of her dodging the weapon or preventing it from sinking to the hilt in her chest.

Except. Nefertiti was too fast, her belt too potent, even for the blood of stars when it was in the hands of a chair-bound boy. She moved as swiftly as the Nile over a cataract, a hippo lying in wait, and she slit his throat with his own dagger of precious star blood that she plucked from the air. The cry of triumph was hers.

Except. She didn't know how far he'd gotten in his experiments to restore vitality to his useless limbs, and she didn't see the odd wisps floating from his mouth, grotesque and open even as his life's blood drained. Which was just as well. Disconnected from his body that never quite moved when he wanted it to, Tut's shadow did what he could not. It strangled Nefertiti and left her there on the ground, the two of them curled in struggle, even in death.

Despite his sickly nature, Tutankhamen's death at nineteen was still unexpected. His funeral was rushed, and his mummified body placed in the tomb meant for Nefertiti, as she had promised.

The woman of the ancient eyes, Penthesilea herself, unbelted the queen, her glittering eyes hard as she failed, yet again, to stop the rise of men. After the official rites and ceremonies, Penthesilea, disguised under the mask of the jackal-headed Anubis, sealed the two of them in the tomb together, enemies in life, enemies in the afterlife.

With her fingers, she traced the ouroboros and left the dagger inside of the mummy's case, resting on his wrapped body. A warding spell kept grave robbers from finding the inner chambers for thousands of years, until another scion of the Order uncovered its secrets and tried to take the treasures under the guise of science! And progress! Howard Carter in the 1920s was just a glorified grave robber, stealing for men and for himself.

Tut's shadow, however, was free to nurture his new secret order of men. It was free to riot emotions and shadow behind those he uplifted to power. His experiments on immortality might have failed, but only just. He had a new life, a second life. And Nefertiti?

She had nothing but a name and a pretty face.

14

I gripped my arms tightly around my body, holding myself together. Otherwise I was afraid I'd fly into pieces.

Back. I was back on Earth. My body felt heavier, gravity-bound. Deprived, almost. The magic was so much weaker here than on the Egyptian plane. Except, it was *different*.

I could sense something odd, something I'd never felt before. It almost felt like vibrations in decay, like dating ancient objects using radiocarbon half-life. For a moment, I was reminded of what it felt like to see Tutankhamen's shadow, except these vibrations were past the point of power. There was no return.

I turned my head slightly, my eyes closed, searching for the source. But it was gone, diffused, impossible to locate. *The smell of fresh sneakers, the swiftly moving tilt and roll of a skateboard, zebra-striped gum popping in my mouth, a crash, hard concrete, sharp pain.*

I frowned. What in the world?

Romaine was next to me, back to his normal, suave-self, dressed in fitted slacks and a button-down shirt with the top two undone. His gray-flecked hair was slicked back in a perfect wave, his horns hidden or gone. The only thing different were his eyes. He and I both knew too much about each other now. What the other one was capable of—and what we were not.

"Bernadette," he said, as if sensing the shift, too.

"We're not talking."

He sighed, genuinely annoyed at me for being furious with him. "I get it. You didn't want me to kill the crazy man hell-bent on world destruction, but this is important."

Crazy or not, he never should've taken justice into his own hands like that.

"What?" I said flatly, wondering if I even trusted him enough to confide anything.

"The world is going to be different. Too much magic has been released—from you, from Simon. It only remains to understand how it has changed."

"I have to find my family," I said, looking past him at the beautiful town of my birth, of Bordeterre. I couldn't meet his eyes. I didn't want to. I knew I was afraid I would see a mirror of my own soul in them. "I have to make sure they're okay."

"Then go. But don't be fooled."

I didn't ask what I was supposed to be on guard for. Anything. Everything. "Where will you be?" I asked instead.

"Here. For now." He turned on his leathered-heel and strode to Au Bistro, as if he were merely going to his place of business to inquire about the headcount for the evening. In his hand, he carried the flaming sword. I didn't ask for it. Romaine was a Duke of Hell. If ever I forgot that he wasn't a tamed beast, I was delusional. And demons of hell, from dukes to cockroaches, didn't give up power.

How could I ever go back to normal after my time in the Outer Planes? How could any of my family understand me anymore? Mon Dieu, what would I say to Amandine the next time I saw her? It felt as if every last bit of my humanity had been stripped from me, flayed like the skin of a fish, and now I was left with only the barest, rawest bits of myself. I dreaded looking her in the eyes, and I could no longer imagine the simplest of pleasures, like ordering pizza for game night and pretending it was any old summer night.

A man bumped into my shoulder, throwing me back a step. I prepared a sharp word—I was in the depths of my despair, here!—but he was muttering to himself, wiping crumbs off his mouth, and completely oblivious. He kept wiping and wiping, muttering, pulling out a baguette and immediately throwing it to the ground. Still, he couldn't get the crumbs off his mouth.

Around the square, I noticed other odd things I couldn't figure out. A woman kept falling asleep in the middle of the sidewalk, waking up with a start, only to fall right back to sleep. I went over to her, if only to call her family or someone to come help her. She was clearly narcoleptic. But when I reached her, the woman scolded me, slapping away the hand that had shaken her awake. Then she immediately slumped back down and snored loudly. Nothing I did could pull her out of it, and the pit in my stomach deepened.

Something was off. It all felt wrong, and I was too afraid to find a newspaper or a phone with internet access to find out how exactly. It would only confirm what I already knew —I had changed the world. Or rather, my blood had changed the world. After everything I had done, I found it hard to believe my blood could change things for the better.

I began to run.

"Where are you? Where could you be?" I muttered to myself, looking just as wild as everyone else on the street. That was the small mercy. The only one afforded to me.

My feet pounded rhythmically, like I was just out for a morning run, all the way to Anouk's apartment. Had they gotten back safely? Were they still in Paris? I pictured the Knights Templar with their shining vambraces and demonic attacks. What world was this? A liminal, in-between world, partially of my creation and partially of theirs? Or, and here I freely admit I let myself hope, had Blaise, Anouk and Sophie with her belt done the impossible? Had they reigned in the Knights, and whatever weird was happening in Bordeterre merely a little aftereffect of my blood splatters, perhaps magnified because we were a border land? Magic was more flexible here, so it would stand to reason my blood would have had a greater impact in this vulnerable place. The rest of the world might be just fine.

Stop it, I shook myself. *It does not a whit of good to speculate. Not yet. Wait to find them.* But I couldn't, or maybe wouldn't, stop myself from hoping. I took the centuries-old steps above Anouk's occult shop two at a time, fumbling in my pocket for the key to her apartment. It was wild to think that it was still there, waiting to be used after traversing the realms. I didn't hear anything or anyone behind the door, and I dropped the key twice due to my fingers shaking so violently. Finally, I got the ancient lock to groan open.

Her apartment was untouched. A cold cup of lavender tea sat in the aluminum sink. I nearly picked it up and warmed it on the stovetop just to wrap my hands around the mug and feel for a tiny second as if everything was normal.

The kitchen smelled faintly of sea bass, as if they'd been here recently. The last time I'd seen Anouk and Sophie, we were sitting in a café in Paris with Blaise, so this gave me hope. The cold cup wasn't from before our trip to UFOPP headquarters in Juf. It could have been from this morning.

I felt their vibrations before I heard them coming up the stairs. My heart leapt into my throat. They were here!

The first thing through the door was Anouk's frizzy hair, and I nearly hummed in relief at the sight. They were really here.

"Anouk!" I cried, full of delight. I ran to embrace my cousin who promptly screamed and tried to faint. Sophie caught her and barreled through the living room, lugging Anouk to the couch where she deposited her. Clarette trailed behind, and I realized it had been so very long since I'd seen our newest friend. "I'm so happy to see you guys, you would not believe what I've been through. Mon Dieu, look at all of you!" I trilled, so very happy and at peace for the first time in a long, long time.

"We thought you were dead," Sophie said flatly. Clarette shifted her weight, her eyes darting everywhere but me. I swallowed uneasily. Anouk just stared, her eyes round and wide. The thick strap of her silk tank top slipped down, and she automatically pushed it back up without even looking.

"I'm sorry," I said. "I know it's been a few days and I just poof! Disappeared, but I'm not dead. Romaine saved me, and Simon is gone for good. It was his last life, so I don't think we need to worry about him coming back, but we should find Blaise and get something to him. It's a sword. Well, a special sword. I think Ashavan was suggesting he should be the heir to the United Federation, or at least, throw his hat in the ring for president. I have a few more items that need to go into cold storage."

I paused and blinked, utterly confused by their looks of shock and by the very odd way my cousin had to keep pulling up the strap of her shirt as if it didn't fit right. "Anouk, your shirt is doing something weird. Do you want to change?"

"Bernadette," Sophie said, her voice tinged with an edge as sharp as an ice pick. "You've been gone for over a month. The only reason your daughter isn't here, mourning your memory so soon after burying her grandmother, is because we have been attempting to make sure without a body, beyond a shadow of a doubt, that you were, indeed, dead. Do you understand? We. Thought. You. Were. Dead. And in your absence? The rest of the world has changed. Quite dramatically."

"What?" I spun around, taking in each of my friends, my family really, more carefully. It wasn't just the dark nicotine stains on Anouk's fingertips from where she'd clearly been chain smoking; it was the angry red stains on Sophie's cheeks or Clarette's green tinged hair. And beyond what the eye could see, there was something off about everyone's vibrations and energy.

Magic.

I knew it was my blood that had done this. The drops from the orrery had reached Earth. They had splattered too far and wide, their implications barely understood.

"What happened while I was gone?" I asked more slowly, more seriously.

"The best thing we can come up with?" Anouk said while simultaneously trying to push her glasses up her nose and her shirt strap back over her shoulder, "The Templars have used their infernal magic from the Outer Planes to turn the world into a place of black and white. Metaphorically black and white, but also kind of literally."

"I don't understand," I whispered, dread congealing like a hot lump in my stomach. Truthfully, I didn't want to understand. I had done this, and my friends didn't realize the source. Guilt flooded my veins. "What do you mean 'metaphorically, but also kind of literally'?"

"Maybe we should get some tea. Lavender okay?" Anouk suggested. "It's been a very long day and a very long month while we're at it. I'm happy you're back, Bernadette, really, I am, it's just... a cup of tea? How does that sound?"

"Our vices," Sophie snapped over her. "All of our vices are on display and there's nothing we can do about them."

"We think its the seven deadly sins, specifically," Clarette whispered.

Call me jet-lagged from inter-realm travel. It still took me a few seconds of staring at Anouk, forever pushing her shirt strap up, to realize what her deadly sin was. "You're lustful?" I nearly screeched.

"It's been a long dry spell since my separation," she said defensively. "Years-long, in fact."

"As I've told her numerous times," Sophie said, "That is the best sin to have. Any decent looking man walking down the street will jump into her bed the second she bats her eyelashes at him."

As she spoke, I tried to figure out Sophie's sin. Her eyebrows hadn't moved from their downward frown and there was a certain red tinged quality to both her irises, not to mention the blotches on her cheeks.

"Sophie, you've never been wrathful in your regular life. It's the belt of Hippolyta doing this to you. That's all," Anouk said soothingly. "More reason to take it off."

"And then?" she yelled, a decibel higher than I wanted to hear ever again in such close quarters. "What will be my true vice? Pride? Sloth? Greed? There are no good options after wrath. Perhaps I will take and live with my wrath and be wrathful. It feels good to be angry every once in a while."

"But all of the time?" Anouk insisted. "That's not healthy."

"At least it's not envy," said a quiet voice behind us, in the most envious tone I'd ever heard. I turned to face her, to really *see* her. The green tint to her hair. The slick way her eyes darted between all of us. The want in her eyes.

"Mon Dieu, Clarette. I... I'm not sure what to say."

"Yes," she said. "I'm envious. How could I not be? You three are so close, you have so much I don't have. You are beautiful, Sophie, fashionable, sure of yourself, successful, and you keep a string of paramours to choose from every week. We should all be jealous."

"*Merveilleuse.* So I will be prideful if I ever take off the belt."

Clarette ignored that and kept going. "Anouk is so smart, has a loving son, and a business to call her own. Don't even get me started on what Birdie has. And me?" She scoffed and it sounded like the most pitiable thing in the world. "I can change into a dirty brown mouse."

"But I thought you liked being a mouse among lions? Remember that whole speech at Lourdes? You were so brave, as if you were coming into your own skin," I said, feeling desperate to help. This was not how I imagined coming home, and I wasn't equipped for this. The world wasn't equipped for this. I nearly wished for the realm of the mossy cliffs. At least it was quiet there, almost meditative in the clouds.

"And nothing has changed since then. I live off of the charity of my friends with nothing of my own. I am a failure. I failed at the only thing I really tried to be: a wife."

"No!" I insisted. "No life lived is a failure. Just because you haven't done everything you dreamed of doing doesn't make it worthless. I'm sorry we made you feel less, Clarette. You're a part of my family."

Clarette sniffled. "And I will never have children, never a true family of my own."

Sophie roared. "And was it better to have lost a child?"

"Of course not. But at least you loved someone, for a while. Which is worse? To want and not have or to have and lose? You, at least, have your memories."

Anouk looked as if *she* wanted to turn into a mouse and run. I got the feeling this was now a perennial argument. One without an answer. Clarette folded her arms tightly across her middle.

"I'm a forty-seven year old waitress with no prospects, no husband, no children, and no hope of children. That's well and fine for people who don't want children, but I did. I really did. I thought Leon would be enough to fill the gap or that maybe he would change his mind and defy his pride, but he didn't and now I'm left with nothing and no one."

My mouth dropped open in horror. I had no idea what to say to comfort my friend—any of them. Saying sorry seemed a bit like trying to put a band-aid on a geyser. And what would happen when they found out my blood was probably the source of all this misery?

I looked out the window, trying to compute that I had missed a month of life here. Suddenly, it was spring in Southern France. I had indeed been missing long enough for the mistral winds to stop blowing, the chilled ground to thaw, and the flowers to bloom in abundance. Bunches of daffodils popped up among the brown leaves of decay. Pops of color appeared at every storefront, and the air smelled sweet with the fragrance of the flowers. It should have been my favorite time of year, but I feared life would never be the same again. Because of me.

"What about the Templars?" I asked, desperate to stop their bickering. "What have they done with UFOPP's head-quarters?"

"As far as we can tell, they control the world's magical

population. Blaise feeds us information when he can, but they have every headquarters around the world on lockdown. The Cathars are in hiding, and even their compound in the mountains has been commandeered."

"And the non-magical population?" I asked.

"They think it's all a bad dream," Anouk said.

"Basically, they don't understand it. That's all they do is talk, talk, talk about what to do," Sophie said, dismissively. "Instead of realizing this is what we have to live with now." She flipped her long blonde hair over one shoulder. "What's your vice?" she asked me suddenly. "I don't see anything different about you."

"My vice?" I nearly took a step backward, my face flaming hot.

"Oui, we all wear one now."

"Maybe I don't have one to wear because I just arrived. I was in the Outer Realms when the Templars did... whatever they did," I suggested weakly. It was probably because it was my blood and I was immune. I didn't quite think this was the time or the place to come clean about that, however.

Anouk snapped back to the old cousin I remembered and loved. "Birdie! We were so wrapped up in our misery... but you must tell us what happened? Where did you go? What did you do? Don't leave anything out."

I realized I was rubbing the back of my neck where the prickles were. I stopped and let my hand drop. "I was in the Outer Planes when this all happened. I actually made it there and thus, wasn't affected by the new magic."

"It's a theory, at least," Anouk agreed. "But come. You must tell us everything. We were so worried."

"For so long," Sophie said, although it sounded a tiny bit sarcastic. My eyes dropped to her belt, which she protectively put a hand over.

"Has Penthesilea shown her face?" I asked cautiously.

"No."

"Because I found out a heck of a lot more about those daggers and the script on them." Anouk's eyes lit up and her fingers grasped my bicep. "Tell me everything. I need a distraction. I'm hot all the time, I'm basically a living, breathing hot flash, you have no idea, and I can't seem to focus, and I had this thought, if someone sprayed a bottle of whip cream on my skin, it would melt, simply melt, I feel so hot, and maybe, you could even fry an egg on my skin—"

"Whoa, slow down," I said, prying her fingers off, which were, indeed, quite hot to the touch. "One thing at a time. And then, perhaps, let's set you up with a dating app. I know you loathe them, but think of it this way, one look at a potential bed partner, and you'll know immediately what's wrong with him."

"Don't go for the ones with lust, too," Clarette advised. "They're bound to cheat on you."

"Well if it's only a one-night thing," Sophie mused. "I don't see why that matters, although if they did, you could just cut off their balls."

Anouk sunk her head into her arms at the kitchen table, avoiding all eye contact. Both of her shirt straps had fallen past her elbows and seemed to be wiggling in an attempt to go down even farther. "I hate my life," she whispered, muffled.

"Join the club," Clarette said glumly.

"You two have no idea—"

"Enough." I clapped my hands and did a short double-finger whistle. Everyone's attention snapped to me. Even Anouk raised her head.

I took deep breaths, hoping to corral my emotions. It was all for nothing. Simon was merely one head of a massive beast, and like a hydra, there were many more. Worse, some of the heads were regenerating. It had taken centuries of women fighting in the Sisterhood to slow the Order of Ancients down, and in my lifetime, even the damn Templars were back, resurrected to wreak havoc. It felt as if I had utterly failed. I didn't even have the flaming sword. Romaine did. A literal Duke of Hell. That was fine, right? That was all fine. Did I mention that I still had feelings for him? Totally, one hundred percent, completely fine. And if I just kept saying the word fine in my head, it might start to be fine. Darkly, I remembered telling him how the word "fine" was basically the opposite in women's language, but now wasn't the time to dwell so I pushed the memory away. It was wild how life actually seemed simpler in Nimue's realm. It felt so long ago.

"Do you recall the shadow demon at UFOPP headquarters that made everyone scared out of their ever-loving minds?" I asked, not waiting for an answer. Of course they did. "Well, it turns out it was Tutankhamen."

"Like the ancient Egyptian boy pharaoh?"

"Yes, also known as the founder of the Order of Ancients. Thanks to a lot of pharaonic inbreeding to keep the royal bloodline pure, he was born with serious medical problems."

"Right. I believe he had a clubfoot among other physical ailments," Anouk said, uselessly trying to knot her shirt straps together. Gleefully, they kept coming undone and sliding back down her arms to expose her cleavage.

"Why don't you just wear a different shirt?" I suggested. It was so distracting, I didn't know how she managed it.

"Because they all find a way to do something ridiculous," she snapped. "I'm tired of my nice blouses randomly ripping right across the bust or all my buttons popping off. If I wear tank tops, at least they only slide down. They don't get ruined."

"Ah." I blinked. "Well. That does suck." I cleared my throat. "Back to Tut. Oh wait, I forgot to mention Romaine and Simon. And my father. Mon Dieu, a lot has happened."

Quickly, I filled them in on finding my father in the shadow realm and then how that turned out to be a shadow demon impersonating him, how the shadow tried to kill me, and how Romaine came charging in to save me at the last minute. Although I didn't specifically mention the blood and the orrery. That seemed irrelevant. Or I was a big demonic coward. Either one.

"So we went to different planes of existence to try to track Simon and stop this madness. I thought we were coming home triumphant, because Simon is dead and his last life is snuffed out." And here, I winced, recalling the look of indifference on Romaine's face and how, deep down under the shock, I'd actually felt glad about it. "The shadow got away, but without a conduit in Simon, I don't think he can do anything."

"And the shadow was the same one? Tut?" Anouk asked, trying to keep it all straight.

"Yes. He got halfway to figuring out immortality before he was killed by Nefertiti."

"That's what a shadow demon is? An immortality experiment gone wrong?"

"This one was. Even weirder, there are actually lots of immortals running around the Outer Realms, and I suspect, Earth, too. Like Madame Hortense."

"Hm. And the meteoric dagger and ouroboros found in Tut's tomb?"

"An ancient language of the stars. It was on pylons in the shadow realm, too. Romaine claimed that place was created after something called the Colossus of Grief. Oh, and he's a Duke of Hell. Remember the grimoire, Le Dragon Rouge? Belphegor, ambassador to France, demon of sloth? Yeah, that's him."

I could see their heads fairly spinning. Frankly, mine was too. I took a breath. Now, finally, I understood why Maman had so easily called up the demon, Ala, without any protection circle or dowsing rod or anything at all. Why she seemed to know the demon, have a history with the demon. Why the demon taunted her. Because she was a demon. My mother, the unflappable Platonic ideal of a chic, French woman, was a demon.

And so was I.

"Should we go get something to eat? At Au Bistro, perhaps? Romaine is back, too. He might be able to help shed some light and fill in details I forget."

"Shed light on what, Birdie?" Anouk asked. She gave me a hard look, her eyebrows down. "I know what you're thinking. You're thinking the world needs to be saved, still. That you've come back from slaying one monster and want to do it again. Well that's not our reality. Just like the rest of the non-magical world, we've come to accept facts. This is our reality."

"No, it's not," I protested. "I stopped Simon, and we can stop the Templars, too."

"Some of us are weary," Clarette said.

Desperately, I turned to Sophie. "You too? What about war and wrath and glory and all that?"

She shrugged one elegant shoulder up and down, still in her Greek warrior Barbie princess outfit she never took off. "I guess I could be persuaded."

"Great, one person is with me."

Sophie tossed her hair. "One is all you need when it's me."

"If you don't think pride is your next one once wrath wears off..." Clarette muttered, still eyeing her enviously.

Anouk put her hands over her shoulders. "Fine. Let's get dinner. I could use a good meal. Then we'll go from there. This might be our current reality, but I hope it isn't forever."

"Hope is all you need," I promised, willing myself to believe it, too. I made my way to the door, determined to get dinner and try to find a moment of normalcy in the chaos of the day.

Yet, as I passed the lintel from the kitchen to the entryway, my left eye twitched. It reminded me of passing through a cold spot in a lake, psychically speaking. The vibrations hit a second later, those of a half-life decay. *Fresh flowers in one hand, a bottle of wine in the other, a jolt of pain down the arm—the crash and tinkle of a bottle breaking.*

I rubbed my left arm where a sharp pain had flashed down for a second. What the fresh hell did that mean?

15

Au Bistro wasn't what I expected in the least. If I thought it would be austere and quiet, most people hiding in their homes, I was dead wrong. The fragrance of the flowers dripping from every eave was nearly as intoxicating as the swirl of cigarette smoke and the simple pleasure of people out enjoying an evening. While the crowds I'd bumped into on our way were harried and rushed, here the natives clearly embraced their vices. Couples made out over bottles of wine, while others ate gluttonously. Still others seemed to just lounge. Pride? Sloth? I had no idea.

Romaine stood behind the bar, murmuring to his bartender. He looked up as if sensing our presence, which I was quite sure he had. I noticed from across the room that his eyes hadn't lost their golden luster.

He gave bisous to all of the women, lingering over my mouth between two cheek kisses. Had it only been an hour ago I'd seen him? It felt as if I'd condensed a whole life since then. I still had whiplash.

"Hungry, my little bird? I came back famished, myself."

"Yes. Everything on the menu," I said, only half kidding. "And a fine bottle of wine."

"Done."

"Also, I wanted you to explain what happened and tell them about the sword—"

Here, Romaine's face changed, strangling the rest of what I was going to say. "Do not speak so loudly here, Bernadette. This is not the world you knew when you left."

"Which is why we're trying to gather here and discuss it."

He looked around the cozy room, a small fire in the hearth and nearly every table filled. "Go find a spot in the back. I'll bring an extra table and chairs. D'accord?"

"Oui, d'accord," I parroted back.

We found a dark, quiet corner near the kitchen, well away from everyone else. It didn't have the charm of a spring-time patio or the cozy interior, but it would do for secrets and plots. Romaine appeared, rapidly ordering a waiter to set the table and then shooing him away as he poured the rosé himself. I watched with my mouth watering as the dark pink liquid splashed into the glasses, frosting the outside and smelling thickly of blackberries. Anouk had him light a cigarette and put it directly in her mouth as she kept herself decent. Finally, she took a long drag, enough to make her eyes roll in the back of her head. Romaine finished the cigarette for her.

"Apparently, we no longer keep a menu," he said, smoke curling around his crown of gray hair, spiked now in a way that mimicked the horns I'd seen in other realms. "It's too hard for the staff, and my head chef only cooks what he wants when he wants. A most prideful, little man. All of that is to say, I hope you like cherry-smoked duck."

"Sounds great. We're just hungry."

"I hope you aren't expecting anything interesting to go with it. He's put the sous chef in charge of the small plates so he can focus on his ducking masterpiece. Are soggy frites okay?"

"Yum," I said half-heartedly.

After we all clinked glasses, cheersing, *Santé*, and Sophie only grunted once to complain that we hit her glass too hard, we got down to business.

"For the precious few that remember the days of the Occupation, it is beginning to feel similar," Anouk began.

I watched as she tried to take a drink, but she kept having to stop, her glass half-way to her mouth, to push up her shirt. Finally, after five or six tries, she gave up and grabbed the wine stem, slurping it down as quickly as possible, which her shirt took as an invitation to expose her no-nonsense nude-colored bra. I tried really, really hard not to laugh, but a small chuckle might have escaped.

"Would you like me to find somebody to take care of that?" Romaine asked her, quite seriously.

For a moment, Anouk's face lit up. "Do you think that would be the end of it? One time?"

"No. But if, for some reason, you were magically satisfied with some wild, one time experience and your lust disappeared, very sad by the way, you would most likely develop a new sin." At the drooping look on her face, he said, "But, I'm sure you could manage the one you have better. Look at the couples here, indulging in their lust. You don't see their clothing flinging themselves off their bodies."

We all glanced around, our eyes finding the couples Romaine nodded to.

His voice dropped a decibel, barely above a whisper. "Just by the act of grazing another's inner arm with their fingertips, sensually sharing a bite of food from the other's fork, leaning down to whisper in each other's ears, any of these acts help manage their symptoms. They indulge, Anouk. That is the cure. As much as the Templars would hate to see it, chastity and temperance are not the answers to life's sins."

Romaine's voice had become silky smooth, and I noticed all three of us had leaned forward, like sunflowers rotating toward the sun. Anouk was even drooling a little from the corner of her mouth. Finally, she cleared her throat.

"Not a demon."

Romaine sat back, his arms crossed over his chest and a smile playing on his lips. "I would never."

"Just a regular, human male."

"As normal as they come."

Anouk sighed. "Well, it wouldn't hurt to talk to someone. You know. For a cure."

"That's the spirit. Ah, our duck has arrived."

All was well and quiet for a moment as we each took a moment to feel normal. Sip our wine, eat luscious duck, and bask in each other's company. It might have been less than a week for me, but in some ways, it also felt like a century since I'd seen my friends and had a civilized dinner. Even Romaine sat and indulged for the entire meal, which he normally didn't do. I asked him about it as he snapped his fingers for a waiter to bring us espresso and a fresh strawberry tart with vanilla-flecked pastry cream and apricot jam to make the fruit shiny.

He looked sheepish. "Yes, well the magic feels very heavy here. It's not at all like I'm used to. Do you remember being on certain planes and the magic feeling different? That's what's happened here, and even I am not immune to its bidding. You're lucky I'm not curled up on some couch sleeping."

"I didn't realize a Duke of Hell was ruled by such things."

"Everyone has rules, my little bird. C'est la vie. But you, you seem fine. No vices, I take it? How interesting."

I gave him a very nasty glare before all of my friends could look at me sideways. No, I didn't have a physical vice, because, as I was starting to suspect, I was immune to magic worked with my blood.

"Back to how we are going to live in this world," I said hastily. "What do we do?"

"Is there anything we can do?" Clarette asked simply. "We've been living this way for a month. If something could have been done, I'm sure smarter or stronger people than us would have done it."

"That's your envy talking," Sophie said. "We can do plenty." When she smiled, her incisors flashed sharply.

"I guess we could try to do research on the original Templars," Anouk shrugged, licking her spoon suggestively as she eyeballed the room. "Even if magic has irrevocably changed this world, that doesn't mean the Templars have to be in charge, manipulating it to keep us this way. If we could get rid of them, we could stop the vices from presenting so outwardly."

I couldn't help but grin. My friends were starting to come back to life. I saw their old fervor and personalities shine through. This brave new world the Templars had created during a moment of magical transformation and chaos thanks to my blood had beaten them down, but it hadn't broken them.

"How do we stop them?"

"We can't live this way. It's inhumane. We are not animals, guided only by vice."

Sophie snorted when Clarette said that, however. "I

think this little experiment proves that we are, indeed, exactly that. Animals guided by vice and only a few virtues." She paused, looking around. "Quoi? Just because it's true doesn't mean I want to live this way. I'm tired of the slovenly look of so many of our fellow citizens. C'est un simulacre de justice!" *A travesty of justice.*

"The better question is, what do the Templars want?" Romaine said, guiding us back. "As I told Birdie, I want balance. This is not that, so I will help you put it back into balance." Romaine turned his luminous golden eyes back upon me. "And you? My little bird? What is your endgame?"

I swallowed hastily, the deliciously smoky duck sliding down a bit painfully. "I don't know what you mean. I've only strived to help the world and keep it from evil."

"And yet, you are essentially the world's definition of evil. You are born of a demon."

My anger boiled to the surface. I was too angry to speak. My friends and even Blaise knew to an extent that I was part demon. But Romaine didn't necessarily know that they knew. He was calling me out. On purpose. To make me—or my family—react.

Then, I saw him scan my friends, reading their reactions. He wanted to know what they thought at that moment. Was it okay to be fraternizing with demons?

My anger began to subside, although it wasn't quite fair to use me in that way. But, after all, he was a demon, too. Evil for evil's sake.

"They already know you're Belphegor, Romaine. You can stop pretending."

Clarette reddened and Anouk's hair frizzed a little. Only Sophie could remain sitting so haughty. I admired that about her.

"Is that so?" he murmured, eyes only for me.

"It's so," I replied firmly.

"I see. Well, the place to begin would be the script you've seen in the shadow realm and elsewhere."

Anouk's eyebrows furrowed together. It was one of her life's great mysteries. She was dazzled by the unknown script and that both annoyed and obsessed her.

"The language was called Enochian by those such as John Dee and other occultists. They also called it 'angelic' or 'celestial'. In essence, they believed it to be the language of the angels. They believed it to be holy. To be good. To be the best of all."

"Is it?" I asked, my fact-driven, lawyerly mind at work. "The language of the angels, I mean. The words *best* and *good* are both pretty subjective."

Romaine shrugged and repeated what he said about Nimue in nearly the same tone of voice. "Comme ci, comme ça. To me, it matters nothing."

I felt it again, those unnatural vibrations, that decay. A whisper of some dark dead threaded through my mind. My shoulders involuntarily shivered and my neck snapped up. Silhouetted against the doorframe of hanging wisteria and fluttering green vines stood an elegant woman. She blocked out the sun, but the moment she stepped inside, silk robes swishing around her tanned and toned legs, I knew immediately who she was.

Madame Hortense had actually left Paris. Madame Hortense had come to Bordeterre.

Well, that couldn't mean anything good.

16

Madame Hortense stood in the bistro in my town. And the weirdest part? She didn't look elegant or put together. She didn't look in control of her emotions or anything like herself. In fact, she didn't even have her usual potions and lotions covering up the scars on her face from her time living as Cleopatra the Alchemist, from the time when she found the secret to immortality. They were ragged peaks and valleys, a roadmap to her life, shockingly bare and bright.

Her oatmeal silk dress hung limp and wrinkled, creased in all the wrong places, and it clashed horribly with her skin tone, washing her out completely. She had no gold bangles or rings, no jewelry or adornment of any kind. She was bare. She also looked the teeniest bit livid, as if she couldn't stand the fact that we saw her without her façade. It seemed the Templar curse wouldn't let her hide her true self. Still, she maintained an elegant, supercilious posture. That was who she was at her core.

"What happened?" Clarette asked immediately, a hungry look in her eyes, which I knew was her skyrocketing envy at work. It was giving her strength to see someone once so haughty and high brought down low by this curse.

"Yes, yes, let's just jump to it. Mine is pride. Happy?" She gave a disdainful look down her nose at Romaine who returned it with a grin.

"Bonsoir, Queen of Shadows."

"Belphegor," she snapped.

He waved a hand. "Oh, they all know. Really, I find it much harder to keep secrets in this modern world than it used to be. Don't you?"

She ignored him. "These sins affect us each in different ways. I can't manage to keep my hair to lie flat, my nail lacquer to stay unchipped or my true facial scars to remain hidden. Is that what you wanted to hear?"

"Honestly? I haven't thought about you at all since I returned to Bordeterre," I said carefully, failing to mention that it was the Outer Planes I was coming back from and not just her shop in Paris.

That comment alone made Madame Hortense's typically composed face flush bright red in every place except where there were streaks of scar tissue. Those remained white.

"Not to be rude, but why are you here?" I asked. "Paris is the epicenter of your world, and we're quite provincial here. According to Parisians, at least. It must be important if you've made the trip."

"You haven't been following the news."

"Been sort of wrapped up in our own thing," Anouk said, snappishly. She was fanning herself with one hand and keeping her shirt up with the other.

"How very narrow-sighted of you. Lust, is it, Anouk? No surprise there," she said, sitting down and pouring herself a large glass of rosé and gulping it down. Tendrils from her loose, uneven chignon bun kept falling out and sticking to her sweaty face. "Where there is news, there is magic."

The seemingly simple sentence caught me off-guard. "What news? And why are you so interested? Is it Divineress business?"

"If it were Divineress business, it would be none of yours, but since you have taken an interest in the Sisterhood and the Queen has come to one of your own, I felt that your involvement was not as odious as it might once have been. Perhaps it is even preferable over involving my witches. I do hate to put my girls in harms' way."

"How wonderful for us," I said dryly, remembering how often she'd sent Geneviève to the Outer Planes in her search for more magic. If that was her idea of keeping her witches out of harms' way, I didn't want to know what harm meant to her. She had, after all, killed the strigoi every time she needed to send her to the Outer Planes. Or Infernal Regions, as they called them. I remembered the library at the Chateau Plaisir, how Geneviève accused her of burning her, of suffocating her, of slitting her throat, every time she needed her to die long enough to ascend.

"News," Hortense repeated, flipping her large-screen phone around for us to see. It was the front page of the digital edition of the French newspaper Le Monde and Le Figaro. Both were in near hysterics with all the changes, although no one on the non-magical side was sure what to call these new tics, or even what they were.

"It's not exactly news that the non-magical world has noticed," Sophie said with a sneer. "How could they not?"

Hortense gave her an exasperated look. "Obviously, I am not referring to that." She scrolled with a finger and clicked on a smaller article at the bottom of the front page. It was about strange occurrences clustered around different towns all over Southern France. A reporter was connecting dots, drawing conclusions, theorizing about the recent events. He never overtly said the word magic, but it hovered in between the spaces all the same. There were tales of misery, disaster, death. Sorrow was interwoven into our human lives, daily even, but this was on another level. "There has been a flurry of baneful activity ever since you left my shop in Paris. I smelled the magic in the air, I smelled your blood, Bernadette. What did you do?"

"I killed Simon," I said matter-of-factly.

Madame Hortense's face went slack. For the first time in our acquaintance, she was shocked. Not even when I saw her hidden, supposedly invisible, ouroboros sign, did she look this surprised.

"Simon de Montfort has lived his ninth life?"

"Yes."

"How? Did you go there or did he come back?"

I waved away her questions. I'm sure she'd hunger to know. "The specifics aren't necessary."

"The devil is in the details," she countered, glaring at Romaine.

He gave her his most charming smile and refilled her glass of wine. "And we are very detail-oriented," he finished for her.

"When we were closing in on Simon," I began quietly, staring straight into Madame Hortense's eyes and willing her to see that I was offering something important here. I was offering information. "He took this net, this unbreakable net of legend that he'd crammed full of magical arti-facts, and he threw it. At the time, I wondered if he had a specific destination or if the objects would simply scatter. Now that I'm seeing this article, I think we have our answer."

"Yes," she said, slowly playing with the condensation on her glass. When she looked up, an unseen gesture passed between us, and I knew she would share information as well. "Geneviève always begged to be helpful. She insisted I try various techniques of death to see which, if any, were more effective. It was her wish to continue to travel, to push the bounds of science and magic. To have her name as the one who risked it all to find new avenues of discovery. She was hungry and I'll admit that I used that hunger in her and fed it, but never against her will."

"I guess we'll never know where the truth lies, although I'd hazard to guess it is somewhere in between."

"Indeed. I had a feeling she was meeting someone in the Infernal Regions, someone who had to be helping her. I had no idea it was Simon de Montfort until she revealed it to us. I just knew she was keeping secrets, both about her partner and the objects she tried to keep hidden from me. The bone spear, for one. Simon must have found that and given it to her. Bone spears like the one she used haven't been seen in our realm since the prehistoric era of mammoths and Neanderthals and Cro-Magnon."

I was tempted to pour her another glass of rosé to keep her talking, but Sophie, smart, beautiful Sophie, did it for me. Madame Hortense didn't even seem to notice. She just kept sipping.

"So," I prompted. "Simon was going around collecting magical objects. For himself or the Templars or both."

"Essentially, he was equipping his army. Remember, the Templars are merely an offshoot of the Order of the Ancients. As distasteful as you find the Amazon queen, and me for that matter, we, at least, know who our true enemies are. We also know that previous enemies make good bedfellows when their interests align."

As if that was the moment I'd been waiting for, a decision snapped in my head. We might go back to being adversaries in the future, but at this moment, war made strange bedfellows, and we were absolutely at the edge of war. Quietly, I pulled out the dormant piece of obsidian I'd been carrying with me since Juf. The missing whole to the piece of glass Maman had left in her perfume bottle. The object that had helped propel me to the Outer Realms or perhaps just focus my energy and vibrations into the correct place.

"Birdie, what is that?" Anouk asked, jumping a little, reacting in some way to its psychic signature.

"The obsidian mirror at UFOPP that was in cold storage. Ashavan took me to view it. He said past presidents claimed to have seen shadows moving inside, but others had scoffed and outright denied it was anything but a shiny piece of black rock."

"But you saw something."

"Yes. I saw shadows moving. And the glass shard my mother left me fit into it perfectly."

Anouk pulled a giant tome out of her bag and began flipping through the pages. So some things hadn't changed. That was good to know. She paused over a few lines. "It was owned by John Dee. Correct?"

I nodded, and then hastily said out loud, "Yes," since Anouk still hadn't looked up. "He was the court occultist and a spy for Queen Elizabeth I of England. But the mirror came from looted booty from a Spanish ship carrying Aztec gold," I remembered. "Dee didn't make the mirror or anything."

"No, but he used it to scry. He thought he was speaking to angels, but it really provides a glimpse into the shadow realm. And here it says he also found some sort of wax tablets with sigils on them from 1347. Wow, John Dee also owned the Sworn Book of Honorius. It is considered the first medieval grimoire and has the first reference to the Sigillum Dei, the sigil of God used by Dee on the wax tablets he kept with the mirror."

"It's all right here," I whispered. "We're on the cusp. I can feel it."

Anouk finally looked up. "Did UFOPP have those wax tablets as well?"

"I'm not sure. I don't think so, though. At least, not on display. The mirror was held between the hooves of these massive rams. Does this mean the British Museum has a fake one?"

Romaine snorted. "Oh yes, by their own desire. The director nearly choked to death on his own spittle when he accidentally summoned a demon by using words of power known to the East while holding it."

Instantly, I recalled the fight against the Templars when Factotum members began shouting *abracadabra* and not in an ironic way.

"He then literally died," Romaine continued, "when the demon ate him."

"Humans really shouldn't go around waving sticks and shouting words they find silly out of a want to amuse themselves. That's the best way to get eaten by demons," Hortense said flippantly. She was on her third glass of wine and clearly not dealing with the new world order very well. "Good riddance."

"What are you suggesting we do?" I asked her. "Go to all of these places and hunt for magical objects? Fight the Templars for possession? It's going to be like a thousand needles in a million haystacks."

"I think we should be more systematic," Anouk offered. Even her shirt seemed to be hanging onto her words for a moment, barely struggling to undress her. "There was also a very strange manuscript, one called the Voynich Manuscript. It has never been deciphered, except by John Dee to say that it looked like an 'angelic' script."

"Enochian, you mean," I said, starting to understand why Anouk thought this was all connected and important. "Like Romaine said. The language in the shadow realm and all over the meteoric daggers is Enochian."

"I think we need to read this Voynich manuscript and see if we can't get to the crux of the issue before heading off into imaginary battle or worse, very real, battle."

"That sounds like a very Anouk thing to say. Brava."

"Thank you."

"I'm not sure it was a compliment."

"Why not? Research should always come first and guns a-blazing, second, if at all."

Just then, as if fate had been tempted into laughing at us, a chill settled through Au Bistro. Romaine and I were the only ones to jump to our feet, staring wildly around. The rest of the restaurant continued their meals, but I knew better. Romaine knew better. Madame Hortense probably knew better, too, but she was dripping the last of the rosé into her glass.

Something was here.

It was there and not, a creature, solid and real, but hard to lock onto. It capered and danced between the interplay of light and dark, and while its vibrations were crystal clear, I couldn't quite figure out who—or what—it was. I thought about throwing arrows or chains or any of my usual tricks, but I didn't want to hit some unsuspecting diner.

I don't know how he did it, but Romaine saw it. He bellowed, "An udug, in my restaurant? I don't think so."

The thing itself was an interplay of light and dark, its

voice poison, its bearing hard to look at directly. It was absolutely not like the shadow demon, but it was still hard to keep in my line of vision, which is probably what made it so terrifying to humans for centuries. Udugs had been terrorizing humans since ancient Mesopotamia.

Romaine snapped his fingers, no longer feeling the need to mess around with dowsing rods for my benefit, I guess, and the beast was suddenly... there. Just there, standing on a small bistro table, snarling. I still didn't understand exactly what an udug was beyond a scary demon, but whatever the hell it was, ugly was at the top of the list. Maybe it wasn't the demon of anything. Just a monster. Maybe all demons were just that: monsters. *No, Birdie. Stop going there.*

It had a collar of interlocking lapis lazuli and carnelian stones and carried a leather handled flail with large knots in each of the straps. His bottom fangs stuck out over his top lip, which was gray like the rest of his skin. He cracked his flail on the table and roared, his pinprick eyes not exactly looking for anyone in particular, just a quick meal. That was a small comfort, however, when it locked onto Anouk. I panicked. There was no way I could let loose fire or arrows in this small space.

Salt. I needed salt.

Sophie pushed Anouk aside and lunged at the udug, pressing the button on her lipstick dagger, switchblading it out. She twirled the blade between her fingers in an impressive display of skill until the udug threw her to the side like a gnat.

Clarette squeaked and grabbed the arm of Anouk. Together, they huddled under a table while I searched frantically for the frequency of salt. I could take it from the duck and the frites as I'd done with Fabien, but—damn it! Just throw all the salt!

Pieces of smoked duck, fistfuls of fries, even the gorgeous salted butter d'isigny all hurtled toward the monster. That caught his attention, but it wasn't until the salt shakers followed, flying as a unit of possessed condiments through the air to smash directly into his face, that he stopped in his tracks. The demon howled, scratching at its eyes and face as its skin began to sizzle and warp, exactly like a slug under salt. The creature flailed, flinging chairs and flipping marble-topped tables without a second's thought. He was going to kill one of us accidentally, which also was no great comfort.

Finally, Romaine put it out of its misery and called the chaos to a halt. In a deep baritone, he intoned, "Abito, Zoxen inferni."

The udug exploded into demonic-smelling dust and disintegrated. This demon was much bigger than the cockatrice and it rained demonic dust for a full minute. We were covered in the black soot, stinking of rotten eggs. Of sulfur. Of fire and brimstone. No one was left in the bistro except for us, as most of humanity, extremely gun-shy to anything that reeked of magic due to recent events, had evacuated the moment Romaine had yelled *udug*. Not that I could blame them.

"That was a tad overzealous, don't you think?" Romaine asked, attempting to brush off the black powder as the rest of us merely attempted not to vomit. Clarette and Anouk did not make it, running to the nearest trash can and aluminum wine cooler respectively with their mouths covered by their hands in a hopeless gesture. Sophie looked nearly green, but as for Madame Hortense and I, we smelled this stink of demons and magic much too often to go around upchucking at its stench.

I shrugged. "I think it was exactly the right amount of zealousness."

Sophie nodded approvingly. "See? That's when you go guns a-blazing," she told Anouk, having to swallow back her nausea a few times to get the words out.

"I guess I agree in such an instance," Anouk allowed, still wiping her mouth with a discarded cloth napkin on the floor. She weakly felt around for her purse and emergency stash of Clorox wipes and Purell.

I turned to Madame Hortense. "We're clearly not going anywhere without salt and a lot of it. Can you make little salt bombs? But of course you can! You're Cleopatra the Alchemist. Make 'em tiny."

"What are you saying?" she asked irritably, clearly not used to drinking so much, or perhaps not used to slaying demons on a wine-filled belly. Again, I couldn't blame her. I tried not to drink and drive away demons, either.

"I'm not asking. I'm telling you to make us demon-neutralizing weapons. Do you need a lab? Because all we have is Anouk's shop and kitchen."

"I'm so glad we cleared that up."

"Not mine," Sophie chimed in. "I highly doubt I'd pass inspections if we're manufacturing magical salt bombs in my café, but you can still take all my salt. It's as pure as it comes."

Something electric passed between the two women as they headed out to Café d'Oc, Clarette reluctantly tagging along behind. Romaine had already harangued his waiters back inside and was ordering his people to clean up, preferring to sit at a table with a bottle of wine from his reserve stock, trying to come back to some sort of equilibrium as he rubbed circles around his temples. This was entirely too much excitement for a demon of sloth, but I knew he'd be here when I needed him. No matter how much he hated to actually move and do things, he understood that things would never get better otherwise.

But why should I take his side and not a different demon? What separated us from the udug? Was murderous intent the only line? And hadn't we both killed in the past few weeks?

"Birdie," he called me over. "I have made a decision. I will not be going with you this time. I am staying in Bordeterre. The spaces between our realm and others have always been wavering here."

"Because of my mother's descent."

"Correct. This is not your fault, of course, but I will stay behind to keep any demons that come through under control. They smell prey, which, unfortunately, wafts straight from Bordeterre."

I squeezed my eyes shut. "I understand. Keep everyone safe here at the hellmouth."

He looked amused for a moment, swiping a piece of dark gray hair over his forehead. "Hellmouth? Hm. Not quite, but close enough."

We left the mess behind, people returning to their dinners as if nothing extraordinary had happened, their deadly sins driving them like the deepest of instincts. As we walked, I whispered to Anouk, "The obsidian scrying mirror isn't the only reflective thing. My father used to watch the world from the shadow realm using a shard from a mirror. It was the only way to view our world from there, and it was given to him by his ancestor, our ancestor, the Lady of Shalott."

"What?"

"Seriously."

"Is it a coincidence or an actual connection? It's not like

there's a piece missing out of the obsidian mirror to connect the two."

"You know that saying: if you hear hooves, you shouldn't suspect a zebra, because it's probably just a horse?"

"Vaguely," she waved a hand.

"Well, I think it's probably the opposite for us these days. Always expect to see a fucking zebra, Anouk."

17

We hustled back to Anouk's occult shop, still hungry since our dinner ended up on the floor at Au Bistro covered in demon ash. At least Madame Hortense had enough presence of mind to grab another bottle of wine, which she uncorked as soon as Anouk locked the door behind her. The shop had the familiar scents of incense, of sage, sandalwood, and frankincense. I breathed in the homey, earthy smell and let my eyes droop, relaxing for the barest of moments. Yes, things were in motion, and it felt like I'd gone from the frying pan to the fire, but we were still standing. We still had hope.

Anouk paced frantically, her flowy blouse toppling stacks of tarot cards as she swept back and forth. "Romaine said it mattered nothing to him about the language of the angels, but he knows way more than he's letting on. Don't you realize?" She didn't pause for one of us to answer, which was just as well. "Everyone so quickly forgets; he's *Belphegor*. He's one of the fallen angels. He's Belphegor. He knows the language, literally. Comme ci, comme ça, my ass. You know who uses that phrase? Only tourists. And Belphegor is the biggest tourist here. Technically speaking. His real home? Hell."

I bit my lip. Now that I knew exactly what he was, what he was capable of, I was struck by how I hadn't noticed the way his easy grace hid the walk of a demon. Of a predator. Perhaps 'hid' wasn't the right word. Simply put, I was blind when it came to him or any man I was romantically interested in, because, well, I hadn't been with anyone since Matthew. That languid movement. The easy charm. It was too perfect. Too wonderful. Speaking of which, when would I start to develop more of that charm as part-demon, or was this as good as it got?

"I have so much trouble deciding how much to trust him. He did literally risk his life to save mine over and over again. As a demon of sloth, I think we should consider that a pretty big deal. But he kept the flaming sword for himself, and he doesn't want to talk about it. Sloth or not, the man moves quickly and ferociously when he needs to. When he snapped Simon's neck, I was surprised not to see the bones pulverized into dust by the sheer force."

"I vote we don't trust him at all," Madame Hortense said. "I've tangoed with that monster in every century, and in every century, he has nearly killed me. It is only through the grace of my intelligence that I've managed to outwit him this long. Now, are we going to find whatever is creating the misery that floods this region or not? It has an epicenter, somewhere."

"How are we going to do that? We don't even know where to start with the research," Anouk said.

"You need to be naked. Take off your pants."

Anouk stared for a second and then shrugged. "Sounds reasonable." She started unzipping her jeans.

Madame Hortense rolled her eyes. "Get me a copper

bowl and fill it with Holy Water. Water from Lourdes will work, if you have any. I will scry. Clothing is optional, but you do not need to be naked for me to work my magic." She paused, staring at Clarette like a hawk. "You, give me that amulet."

Our eyes snapped from a half-undressed Anouk to Clarette who'd clutched her lapis-colored elfshot amulet to her chest. Her eyes darted to the front door. "But... you gave this to my family. To my parents. To me. It's mine. I need it. It's... it's all I have in life!"

"Irrelevant. I created it, I need it." She stalked over and snapped the chain loose before we could do or say anything. Clarette let out a scream of downright anguish that reverberated through my bones.

"Stop acting like a child. I'm not going to ruin it."

"Maybe you should have led with that," I said angrily. "Like it or not, you're in our house now. You'll have to play by our rules."

"Which are?"

"Civility."

Madame Hortense tilted her head, studying me. The elfshot amulet hung between her fingers. "I do believe you think you're being serious."

"I am, and you better do more than believe it. You better feel it in your bones," I told her. "I am not the woman you met only a few months ago. I am much more than that. Do not test me."

Madame Hortense ground out, her back molars really taking a hit, "May I use your amulet to scry for evil, world-ending Knights before they do worse than embarrass you in public with your sins on display? I swear I will not irreparably harm it, however, we are looking for strong wards and the amulet itself is a strong ward. Like will find like."

Clarette's eyes were flooded with tears. One dropped to her nose, but she nodded, her hands still clutched at the now-empty space on her neck.

"Good. Now get me that Holy Water and copper bowl. While I work, I want you to assemble the rest of the items I'll need to create your... salt bombs, did you say?" She rattled off a list of mundane and fantastical sounding things as she prepared the bowl, wrapped the amulet around her palm three times, and paused, a needle over the pad of her third finger. Then, she offered the needle to me. "Unless you'd like to contribute, Bernadette?"

"I'm good," I said, not taking my eyes from hers. "No need to have you take any leftovers for yourself."

She lifted one shoulder, a smile curling at the edge of her mouth as if she could smell me and the role of my blood in this new world, and pricked her thumb. She let her blood drip into the water, a red bloom, an inkblot, a hope. Then, she began to swing the amulet over the bowl of water, her nose inches from the surface. She muttered, either madly to herself or some sort of trance-inducing spell. I saw nothing in the bowl but her own, murky reflection.

A few minutes later, she stood straight, her mouth grim and set. Clarette held out her hands and Hortense unraveled the amulet and placed it in them. "I have a location. It's not specific, only a city."

"Where?" we asked eagerly.

Her brows furrowed, as if it confused her, too. "Marseilles."

* * *

"THE LAST TIME I was in Marseilles, I broke my favorite dagger. And my favorite nail, come to think of it, while wielding my favorite dagger."

Sophie had gone first in the world's saddest game of woe-is-me. We all held up our glasses and then took a sip of wine in solidarity.

"The last time I was in Marseilles, my friends all abandoned me to go off and save the day," said Anouk.

Another toast, another cheers, another sip of wine.

"The last time I was in Marseilles, my own brother tried to kill me," Clarette said mournfully. A slight pause—it was getting darker by the second.

"That one deserves a shot of something more serious," I said. "Anouk, do you have any of the good spirits around here, or is it just that swill you call brandy?"

"Just the brandy," she said sourly. "And thanks."

Madame Hortense went next. "The last time I was in Marseilles, it was 1720 and I was on a plague ship."

We all stared. I didn't want to come out and say that she had won the woe-is-me game, but I wouldn't want to be anywhere near a plague ship. Or the year 1720 for that matter.

"Well." I shook myself free first. "Go on, then. Tell us about it."

Hortense poured herself another glass. "Not much to tell. Belphegor had stolen my iron mask, and I went to track it down. Much like I'm helping you track down whatever is causing so much misery in the world, or at least, more than usual."

"You're also invested in less misery, so let's not mince words," I said. "More misery, less perfume."

She tossed her head back as if my words were dandelion fluff on the wind. "At any rate, it was my first time with a

Levant plague demon and hopefully my last. Belphegor had asked the demon to infect a ship, which it did, and that led to a fourth of the population of Provence dying. What?" She taunted me. "You thought Romaine was a tame demon?"

I didn't want to say what I was really thinking. *Yes. I did.* Because I thought of myself as one, too. We didn't hurt for pleasure. Deep down, there had to be a thread of goodness in Romaine. Right? If he was a fallen angel, at one point, he had to have been good. And that was all just gone? Poof! How was that possible? Couldn't some of his goodness, his angelic side, remain?

"Did you get your mask back?" Sophie asked.

"I did get my mask back, and it was worth the cost."

"Because others paid it," I pointed out.

"Oh! Mon Dieu!" Clarette suddenly squeaked. "Do you remember where my brother was holding me hostage with Geneviève in Marseilles?"

"Yes," I began. "It feels like another lifetime ago, although I know intellectually it was only a few weeks. Well, longer for you guys. We went under the Chateau d'If, right?"

"Correct."

I couldn't fathom it at the time—who would have created that chamber of fear filled with magic that tasted of bitter orange piths, thick and fuzzy? How? Why? I never understood how it had gotten there to begin with.

"I saw other parts of the chateau when..." here she took a moment to swallow and steady herself before saying his name, "when Albert was... well... occupied. Simon wasn't the only man Geneviève was with. Romantically."

"Ah."

"Oui," she said, burning red on her cheeks, the poor, repressed woman. "I saw all sorts of weird things, including crumbly ruins that looked faintly Greek in nature, and when we got back, I couldn't help but get sort of manically interested in it. I mean, I thought I was going to die. I got away from Leon just to get burned by my own brother."

"Oh, Clarette. He was being used by the strigoi. But it was so frightening down there. I'm sure you have some PTSD from it. I'm sure we all have unworked-through trauma."

"Well, it turns out, Marseilles is the oldest city in all of France and one of the oldest in Europe. It was founded by the Greeks as a trading post. I mean, there were the natives living there already, although there is some debate among scholars as to whether there were Celtic natives or Gallic natives in the area at this time, but even the origins of the names are all really obscure and it's a big fight, academically-speaking, basically all the time. I don't think that matters much to us, getting in the weeds like that, because it's the Greek invaders we care about. I know. Weird to think of the Greeks as invaders and not the Romans, but they were doing it, too. Invasion: it's human nature."

Our mouths hung open. Anouk in particular looked a little on the ruffled side, like maybe her new deadly sin was about to be envy.

I snapped out of it first. "Is there anything you can't do, Clarette? Bake better than Sophie. Sorry, Sophie. Research like Anouk. What? Don't look at me like that. You heard her. And outwit me before deciding to help me with Le Dragon Rouge. You truly sell yourself short."

At that, Clarette positively glowed like an ember. There was a pop! and suddenly Clarette was a mouse wearing a dress. Another pop! and she was back again, this time, without a tinge of green.

If possible, our mouths dropped even wider. Spiders could have nested inside, and we wouldn't have noticed.

"I feel light. I feel the albatross lifted from my shoulders. I feel... marvelous!" She twirled in her dress. "My friends! My life! It's not second-rate! I'm me and I'm fine. I'm going to be fine."

"Your envy is gone," Sophie said, still looking a little on the snarly side. "You figured out how to lift your envy."

Clarette didn't sag or look defeated. She truly looked like a dying woman given a second chance at this world. And for a moment, I think the rest of us felt true envy. Her excitement made her throat vibrate, her words vibrate, most literally. I could see the magic of her newfound self-appreciation spooling off of her.

"Can we get back to Marseilles?" Anouk asked, holding her straps with one hand and fanning herself with her other.

"Désolé. I'm sorry. I just haven't felt this wonderful since banishing Leon, that rat-bastard. What I meant to say is, don't you think this disturbance is something Greek in nature and currently hiding under the Chateau d'If?"

18

Anesidora
  Olympia, Ancient Greece

HER BODY WAS *wet to the touch, still unfinished. Curved shavings of clay lay scattered at her feet. Her arms had been sculpted to rise over her head, her hands clasped, her head turned to the side, eyes closed. They wouldn't open until that breath of air, that spark of life was granted to her.*

The gods crowded in their hall, the long colonnades filled with light and laughter, banners unfurling in the deepest shades of gold and purple. The undercurrent was one of gleeful malice, the anticipation of revenge and humiliation as tantalizing as the morsels of fruit and ambrosia displayed on golden platters.

When Hephaestos carried her out in his arms, his own chiton slipping off one muscular shoulder, they wondered if he hadn't half-fallen in love with his creation already. They smirked and whispered behind their goblets of shimmering nectar, but the giant of a god was used to that and barely noticed. He placed the statue on her wedding dais, arms eternally lifted until given life.

Adorned by quick-fingered Athena, she wore a dark-sleeved chiton, decorated with garlands of stars. Her feet were bare, still made of mud and not worthy of anything. Loose curls hung down her back, held in place with a silver fillet, something too ornate for a mortal. It must clearly be a little joke between gods. Or, they whispered, a gift from the craftsman to an unrequited love. He's rather good at those. Gifts and unrequited love, of course. *They giggled like nymphs, so pleased with their wittiness, not dulled a bit after all these centuries as immortals.*

Athena came first in order to bestow her second and third gifts. The gray-eyed goddess caressed the statue's fingers with her own, imparting the knowledge of needlework and weaving.

Next came Aphrodite, her hips round and wide, her baby on one of them. With the slightest curve of a smile, she bestowed her gift: a single kiss, which shed grace and cruel longing and cares that weary the limbs. The Charities, the Graces, and Queen Peitho of Persuasion came together to offer her gold jewelry while the rich-haired Hours crowned her with flowers.

Then came the last of the gods to offer their gifts. The sly trickster, the god who would steal cows and walk backwards to hide his tracks, the god who never stopped smiling, What did he gift the woman of clay?

Hermes gave her his breath. He gave her lies and crafty words. He ensured she took some of his deceitful nature. He did as he was told. He gave her a voice, but it wasn't her voice. It was his.

And Hermes took the new bride to her husband, a bridal gift of a jar to go with her. There she goes, they said. A καλός κακός. *There she goes.*

A beautiful evil.

19

Rosemary, sage, vervain, and smudges of palo santo all bound by sulfur and a drop of liquid mercury. The resulting capsule was small enough to hide anywhere. Purses, pockets, a locket. I chose to throw a fistful into my bra and every spare pocket I had. We stuffed our socks with amethyst, and onto our skin, we patted black tourmaline that had been ground into sparkling powder and mixed with moon water. We shimmered as darkly as any avenging angel.

Anouk used the powdered tourmaline to line her eyes and make her chest look as if she'd bronzed all day. "Wow," I said. "You look sexy."

"Really? Maybe I should wear this to Au Bistro."

"Not the worst idea you've had."

Why was I so excited? Why did I hunger for this hunt? Surely that said something about my state of mind. What had I kept hearing? The death of my mother, my newly empty nest, becoming an expat, leaving my stable job of decades: any one of these things should have set off alarm bells. All of them within the space of months? Yeah. I shouldn't be this excited to hunt deranged Templar Knights.

But I was.

I salivated for it. I yearned, deeply. Maybe I just wanted to prove I was one of the good guys. What did that make Romaine?

"Hey," I asked, pushing down uncomfortable existential questions, because, duh. It was easier. "Does anyone know what happened to Capitaine Blaise Laurent? This seems like something that would excite him."

"He was helping evacuate the Cathars from their mountain stronghold," Anouk said. "I'm not sure where he is now."

"Nico did the same thing," Sophie said, a bit dreamily. Honestly, really dreamily, in Sophie's case. The woman was usually so matter-of-fact that any bit of daydreaming was basically unheard of. "Helped others, that is."

"Give him a medal, or better yet, make him a chevalier in le Légion d'Honneur," Hortense snapped. "For doing the bare minimum. It is tough for a man, after all."

I had to physically restrain Sophie at that, which would have never happened in my previous life if not for a little pull on her vibrations to slow her down.

"Sophie! Stop, you're going to rip my arm out of my socket," I yelled. "You hate men now, too, remember? The belt? This is like the one thing you have in common."

"She shouldn't speak about Nico that way. He doesn't count. He's a good man."

"Doubtful. At most, he puts on a good act in front of a crowd," Hortense muttered, and it was back to restraining Sophie as her fur ruffled under my hands. She desperately wanted to shift. She couldn't, of course, with her belt on, but oh, how she wanted to.

"We are on the same side," I told them both sternly. "Act like it."

"For now," Sophie growled. Her hair stood out like she'd spent the afternoon with her finger in a light socket, and her lipstick was smudged. But, so was Hortense's for that matter. It was wild to see these two elegant women brought so low by the curse of the Templars. I wondered if it affected the Knights, too, or if they'd managed to barricade themselves off from the effects of the seven deadly sins. Honestly, they probably did and just patted themselves on the back for having no sins; they were the chosen. Men always did that. Look at the Inquisition. Weak men telling themselves how much others had sinned, while secretly being angry at themselves for their own sins. And now the Templars were literally trying to bring the whole messy affair back. It would not surprise me in the least if they would physically begin a second Inquisition into the new world once everyone's sins were cataloged and they pretended they had none, exactly like the first time.

"I'm going to call Blaise and update him. If the Cathars are in hiding, it seems they would be interested in helping. They are neither Order of the Ancients nor the Sisterhood, but this may shift another strange bedfellow to our side. It's time to make them choose."

I left the women to gather up our supplies and went to call Blaise. I didn't know what sort of survival mode he was in. Was he still at his police station in Lourdes covering for the Cathars as best he could? Or was he evacuating the Cathars and keeping them safe, *alive*, in some mountainous overpass? The man had a lot on his plate, but we all did.

He picked up the phone in two rings, his voice even and deep. Very business-like. "Laurent."

"Do you ever look at caller ID?"

Blaise's breath hitched. "Madame, what the actual hell happened to you."

"We're already back to Madame, eh?"

"When one magically disappears, abandoning one's friends after a horrific event during a world crisis? Yes. We are."

"Would it help if I told you I actually got to the Outer Planes and stopped Simon de Montfort, your old partner, I might add, from wreaking more havoc?"

"You better come down to the station so I can question you properly."

"Why? You need to see the whites of my eyes to judge if I'm telling the truth?"

"I'll be here for another hour," he said stoutly.

"Sorry. I'm afraid I'm about to take a trip. Which is why I'm calling, actually. I want you to come."

"Is this quite the time for a vacation, Madame? You may have been off fulfilling some hero fantasy, but the rest of us have been in the trenches on Earth."

"Speaking of that, I am curious what your sin will turn out to be, but alas, it's not a vacation. We think we know where the Templars are, at least in Southern France. Have you been following the news?"

"I always follow the news. I am the news."

"Ah. So you got pride. Interesting. I would not have guessed that."

I heard a muffled noise as Blaise clearly covered the receiver of the phone with his palm and cursed a few times under his breath, muttering and snorting in odd intervals.

I grinned. "Self-loathing, sure. That I could've seen. Gluttony, for punishment, obviously. Envy, absolutely—"

"Madame, where are the Templars?" He returned from his little scream session sounding as composed as usual.

"Will the Cathars come? It's their ancestral enemy, too, you know. We could use the firepower. As they say, the enemy of my enemy is my friend. I think we can be friends long enough to stop this madness."

"I am the Cathar's arm and their will. I am enough."

"No, I really think you're not. Don't let your pride get in the way, Blaise. Whatever they have is enormous. It's emitting misery and death on an unprecedented scale. The object must be found and contained. If need be, I'll even give it over to UFOPP's Antarctic storage."

"Where, Bernadette?"

It wasn't a question, not really. Just an irritated command.

"How are you doing, really, Blaise?" I asked quietly. Ashavan's last moments under the control of the djinn surfaced to my mind and surely to his. Instead of softening Blaise like I'd hoped and making him remember our shared time when we actually worked like a good team, his pride trampled everything.

"I will avenge him, but I need the location. I would say don't bother coming, but I don't know the last time you ever took good advice. Probably decades ago."

"Fine, Blaise. Have it your way. I'll see you in Marseilles." I hung up the phone and whispered. "And hopefully not hell, first."

20

Marseilles was exactly as I remembered. Bright, sunny, briny. The people moved differently, however, and the energy felt off, filled with an undercurrent of tension and fear. The Templars had done this. With my magic.

I still hadn't mentioned the orrery and the way my blood had painted our world into something new, something unrecognizable. Not to my friends, and especially not to my frenemies. Still, I wondered what Madame Hortense understood. Did she know what the Templars used? Some type of spell or artifact?

Instead of taking time to grab something to eat, perhaps finally finishing that bouillabaisse by the seaside, we went straight to the ferries and booked tickets for the Chateau d'If.

Despite having much more experience, weapons, and people with me this time, it felt as if the same pit had opened up in my stomach. Yes, I didn't have the ransom note shell, *Drown after Reading*, ominous and dark, yet so much more was at stake. Pretty much the whole world. And I didn't even know if I was on the right track? Was the object we searched for an ancient Greek relic?

Like last time, the sun set over the waves as we launched off, the last ferry of the day. I could see the jagged oval of the rocky island floating a little distance from the bay. The sky was blue and the sun magnificent, but a light rain began to fall from the heavens. I looked up, shielding my eyes, and tried to let it cleanse me. "Devil's beating his wife with a frying pan."

Even Anouk looked confused and she was used to me. "Quoi? I hope that is another one of your American Southern oddities and not some real thing you're sensing."

"Just an adorable Southern saying," I confirmed, letting the very real chills I was getting roll down my back. "Well, not that adorable, I guess. If the sun is shining and it's raining, then these are her tears."

"Why is it coming from the Heavens then?" Clarette asked.

I shrugged. "I always asked Maman that, too. She insisted it was just a silly saying of our less-than-charming neighbors. But after going through the realms, up and down are not as we imagined them. We're all sort of... tangled together."

I noticed a man standing, looking at the water, his palms on the metal railing. From the back, he was broad-shouldered, tall, well-built for a man with silver hair. I knew the moment he turned around, I would recognize a strong, Roman nose and piercing, glacial blue eyes.

"I'll be right back." I excused myself from the tight group of my warrior women and went to Blaise. Silently, I joined him at the railing, watching swallows swoop for bugs. His presence was exactly as I remember. Solid, warm and real. I wanted to bask in it for a bit. Plus, he was much easier to manage when he was quietly introspective and not sparring with me over legal odds and ends.

And so I stood, just like that, taking in the golden sun dipping lower in complete silence with the good capitaine. Where Romaine could charm a rock, Blaise let silence be his strength. One wasn't better than the other, although I had a feeling both of them would be completely offended if they knew I thought that. They were each other's antithesis.

Finally, I broke the silence.

"You haven't yelled at me for not waiting."

"You already know what I think, Bernadette. Why waste my breath?"

Suddenly, Blaise looked down at me, a full head and shoulders taller than me. I had to tilt my chin to gaze up at him and for a moment, I felt lost. Confused, even. Like I wasn't on steady ground anymore, and things kept shifting beneath my feet. I didn't know what Blaise thought. I could never know. He surprised me all of the time, like when he released his demon, Naberius, from his service without telling his Cathar supervisor. That was wholly unexpected. And now he wished for me to read his mind? No, he insisted that I already knew how!

"I actually don't, Blaise. I have no idea what you think about me." Had I really said that? Was this end-of-the-world type of emotions running through my veins that made me feel vulnerable? Well, it was out there. No take-backs now.

Blaise made a noise, somewhere between a huff and a scoff. Or something else, disbelief, perhaps.

Before he could mount a response, I said, "Maybe it's because you don't even know what you think. Am I getting warmer?" With a small grin, I added, "Ideomotor move-ments, Capitaine. You're the one who taught me about them. Unconscious acts from unconscious thoughts."

I turned to leave him to his study of the swallows and the waves but his fingers clamped around my bicep, hard and unyielding. I caught a glimpse of his Sig-Sauer on his hip along with his meteoric dagger, taken back from UFOPP's storage presumably, or given to him directly by Ashavan before his death. Not a hint of sulfur surrounded him, however.

My eyes went from his hands, still improbably on my arm, up to his eyes. There was usually so little emotion to glean from them that it was a shock to see the conflict.

"Birdie." His voice was low. He blinked. A blanket of pride hung about him, thick as Madame Hortense's. It was harder to see how it physically affected him, except for perhaps a certain hunger in his eyes and a hunch to his shoulders from the weight of his pride. Yet, he still looked battle-ready at all times.

"Blaise?" I blinked, confused, taken off-guard by his voice.

"If you wish to know what I thought, I will tell you. I was worried. No, that doesn't convey how I felt. I was scared. For the first time in years, no, decades, even, I was terrified for someone's safety. You had disappeared right in front of my eyes, and I couldn't do a damn thing to stop it. I couldn't save you, I couldn't go with you, I couldn't do anything. And the thought that I cared enough to want to do something was even scarier. Not just for the greater good or for the world, but for you. Only you."

Something in Blaise's look snapped. His pupils went translucent, and he doubled over, moaning once.

"Blaise!" I threw my arm around his waist to help him stand, but he was already breathing more normally.

"Non, it's fine. I'm fine. I feel great, in fact."

Instantly, I knew what had happened. "Did you seriously

just get rid of your deadly sin?" The man had one little conversation with me and bam. Gone? I don't know whether to be happy for him or annoyed. He'd literally swallowed his pride to reveal his true self to me and in doing so, overcame it. For me. Mon Dieu, now I really didn't know how to feel.

"Merde, I can't believe I allowed my pride to take over. How reckless—we are without backup, going into the unknown, following an instinct with half-assumptions—"

"We did scry so it's not completely instinct," I said, a bit bluntly. "Obviously you don't have to keep going, but we are."

"Of course I must help." Blaise shook out his hands, flexing his fingers and blinking rapidly. He looked woozy on his feet, and immediately gripped the railing, his knuckles white on the metal.

"Madame—"

"Yeah. I think we're past that. It's Birdie or bust."

Blaise lifted an eyebrow. "Fine. Birdie. I apologize for laying that all at your feet. We must focus on the task at hand, personal feelings aside. Of course, I must help," he repeated. "Non. I want to help, but we cannot allow ourselves to become distracted right now. My pride nearly got in the way of everything, dooming us all." He was running a hand through his thick hair, agitatedly attempting to re-focus on the actual job at hand, although I was still reeling.

"Blaise, you don't get to say something grand like that and then just say the conversation is over!"

"I think we have no choice," he said softly, as the ferry jerked to a stop, bumping up against the dock at the Chateau d'If.

21

The Chateau stood exactly as I remembered it, exactly as it had for hundreds of years. Yellowed stone and cobbled ramparts. A golden setting sun. The only thing different?

The stench of dark magic clung to everything. It coated the ground like a blanket, and a thick, invisible mist swirled around our feet. The particles in the air vibrated, making it feel like I was slugging through evil maple syrup. The other tourists glanced uneasily at one another, their conversation unusually muted. Some even laughed nervously and they all stayed clumped together. Except for us. Apparently, we were the professionals. God help us.

Anouk and Clarette stood on either side of me, while Blaise, Madame Hortense, and Sophie in Hippolyta's Belt took the lead. She still insisted on wearing a flowing white chiton and jeweled sandals, but the rest of us all wore sensible tennis shoes, even Hortense. The cost of her pride had indeed brought her low. Blaise, on the other hand, seemed as if the storm clouds hovering over his shoulders had lifted.

I couldn't help stealing sideways glances at him. What

had he meant? Was that a declaration of love? Or just a declaration of no longer hating me? It hadn't felt overly romantic, just anguished, which was Blaise's normal M.O. He'd let me in as a friend, something, it seemed, he probably hadn't done in a long time. I'd bet the last person he let in as a friend was Simon, who turned out to be an ancient lion shifter hell bent on becoming immortal and not afraid to change the world with blood magic to do it. Specifically, my blood magic. Maybe Blaise felt guilty for not realizing it before it was too late.

I was so caught up in my musings that I nearly tripped over the uneven stone ground. Blaise caught my elbow and a hot swoop of confusion settled in the base of my stomach. I needed some control.

"Merci."

"De rien," he replied, already scouting out the landscape, as if he hadn't just touched me and caused an international crisis in my mind.

"Do you sense anything, Madame?" he asked.

I let the 'Madame' comment slide. Some space between us seemed like a good idea, both physical and mental. "Oui. Same spot as last time," I whispered, giving Clarette a glance. She had turned a bit white under her ears, no doubt feeling all the feelings from the last time we were here. "Are you going to be okay to go in? Don't feel pressure. We have plenty of firepower this time."

"Firepower, Madame?" Blaise asked. "I'm not sure what you think this mission is, but it's not an American style cop raid, breaking down the door and shooting first with questions later."

"That's not really how it's done in America either. At least, it's not supposed to."

"This is a fact-finding mission," he continued. "We will

gather information so we can make an informed decision on how to proceed."

"Who invited this wet rag?" Sophie asked, sniffing as she looked him up and down.

"Me," I said impatiently. "Blaise, I understand what would be the best-case scenario here, but we're not in best-case scenarios anymore. We're way past those." Part of me was happy that Blaise was instantly back to disregarding everything I said and trying to insert himself as the leader. He was a natural at it, but this was my mission. The Templars were here with something big. Something dark. The world wouldn't be free from the influx of magic from my blood, but perhaps we could at least get rid of a massive amount of misery. We could stop it in its tracks, whatever it was.

By now, we'd all maneuvered quietly down to the gated tunnel where Sophie and I had found Clarette. It looked unchanged, which was a little worrisome. If there was intense Templar activity, shouldn't it be warded, hidden from the view of tourists with some spells?

I held up a fist, which I thought was the international sign for halt. "I'm going to go first with absolutely no arguments, because I can feel vibrations and—"

With a whoosh, my feet went up and my body went down, and I was sliding, the shock so sudden that I didn't even have time to scream. Where once it was a golden sunset over low tide in the Mediterranean Sea, now it was a tarry black curtain of terror. Finally, I found my voice, but as I was about to scream out of sheer reflex, I knew I had to swallow it down. This was not here before, and it had been so expertly warded—or I had been so expertly distracted—that I hadn't noticed.

I stuffed myself into my protective bubble, *Tengatur*, and

not a moment too soon. Immediately, I came to a stop at a gaping maw of rusted spikes that looked like teeth ready to consume me. Putting my hand over my chest to press against my heart's frantic beating, I rubbed at it to help ease my fright. Luckily, the more I used my protective magic, the easier it had become. Whether it was a case of practice makes perfect or use it or lose it, I didn't know. Nor did I care to pick my cliché. I just knew I had to keep searching for that wellspring of love that powered it more easily, more smoothly, and embrace it.

When I wasn't frightened out of my mind, I scooted on my stomach to the edge of the abyss to see a gold piece that had caught my eye. There was a medallion on one of the iron spikes. The golden coin looked familiar. Two men riding one horse. It represented the poverty they promised to live by when swearing their oaths to the Order. It was the same as the tattoo on the male half of the fornicating couple I kept seeing everywhere. This was a booby trap. A Templar one. The coin must have fallen off one of the Templars who had installed it. My body felt a mixture of elation and terror. I had barely avoided the spikes at the bottom. Not a super sophisticated one, but then again, not many booby traps had to be sophisticated to be effective.

I collapsed the bubble and tried to get a better sense of where I was. If for some heroically dumb reason my friends decided to follow me down, I needed to get rid of these spikes and soon. Was it possible to speed up molecules and thus, the vibrations? I had started experimenting with slowing things down like with Nimue. What if I could explode them? Examining all the edges for ways to possibly blow this place to bits, I thought I heard something, but I couldn't tell from which direction. Screw it. There wasn't enough time to experiment. Like the last time Sophie and I were here, sans spikes, today was not the day to try out shiny new spells. Or powers.

I began cushioning each individual spike with one of my protective bubbles. A couple moments later, I heard a shriek of metal on metal coming from above. Of course one of those beautiful idiots was coming to my rescue. Frantically, I tried to go faster, but there were still a few spikes at the bottom that looked deadly serious. "Duh!" I exclaimed, spreading out a blanket bubble. Why was I individually bubble wrapping them like I was shipping precious cargo across the world?

Only heartbeats later, Blaise arrived in his loud and bright glory, a look of grit and determination on his face as he tried to slow his descent by dragging his sword behind him. So many of the muscles on his biceps were flexed, I wasn't even sure I had the same number of muscles there as he did. I certainly didn't use them like he did.

He bounced into the dome and off of it just as Sophie came tearing down after him using her nails to slow herself, sounding exactly as if she were scratching a chalkboard.

"I told you to stay behind," Blaise said as he dusted himself and examined his sword tip with a grimace.

"And let you have all the fun?"

I interrupted them. "Why did either of you come? What? Is Anouk showing up next?" I tried to imagine my cousin jumping into the unknown. Not that I thought she wouldn't come save me, but it was harder to imagine. I was curious to see it.

"Of course not. I told her to wait."

"Like you told Sophie?"

Blaise scowled harder. He pulled out his cell phone and dialed Anouk.

"I could have done that, you know. Before all of us got stuck down here," I said.

"But you didn't," he said and then boomed into the phone, "Anouk, we're fine. Birdie is fine. I want you three to stay up top and keep an open line of communication. Do not attempt to follow. There's a booby trap at the bottom, and although Birdie has stabilized it for now, I don't know how long her protection will last. Ça va? Bon." He ended the call and then looked at me. "What?"

I had my arms crossed, tapping my toe, but instead of speaking, I just threw up my hands. "Forget it. Now, can both of you manage not to make a ton of racket while we infiltrate a Templar stronghold?"

"How do you suggest we get around the spikes?" Blaise asked. Now that his enhanced pride was gone, he was more open to working together, to hearing ideas. The only problem was, I had zero of them.

Sophie tilted her head to both sides, assessed the angles of the small tunnel we were in, measured both of us up and down, and cracked her knuckles. "Don't make any sudden movements," she said ominously.

"Wait. Why?"

But it was too late. Sophie scooped both of us under her arms and took a running leap, soaring over the spikes that ranged along the ground for at least fifteen feet, and landed in a nearly perfect tumble on the other side, her chiton flaring around her thighs.

"Sophie, that was more terrifying than dropping into an unknown black hole of a tunnel alone."

"Adrenaline is good for the heart," she said. "You're welcome."

Blaise was already prowling ahead, his dagger and Sig-Sauer both out as he crept forward. I don't know if he realized it, but he flinched when he went through a particular bend in the tunnel. I went right up to it and closed my eyes, although I hadn't needed to. The moment I found it, my body felt like I'd been drenched in an icy lake.

It was a cold spot.

Weary feet, unwashed bodies under heavy leather armor. The earthy taste of oregano and the greasy fat of roast lamb, a last meal, still on the tongue, turning bitter.

"Are ghosts real?" I asked finally, the eldritch feeling of horror still strong here. No, it was stronger. This place of horrors had not gone dormant, left alone to its devices. It had changed. And with that cold spot? I'd felt vibrational decay. An ancient Greek soldier had died fighting down here by the psychic feel of it.

"Anything is possible," Sophie shrugged.

"I keep feeling... impossible things." I said this last bit as we sank beneath the familiar words that we'd seen last time: Abandon Hope All Ye Who Enter Here. The giant marble chess board floor had seen better days, and I squeezed Sophie's hand. Last time we were here, we had seen Albert and Geneviève die, although Geneviève's death had been a little less permanent than we'd thought. I said a quick prayer, crossing myself, and hoped they were finally resting in peace.

By the looks of it, large tracks had been left by something that seemed metal, grinding across the floor. We kept moving, all remnants of the fight we'd had vanished and curious markings from whatever the Templars had done unexplainable.

"Do you still commune with Naberius?" I asked quietly. I hadn't seen the demon in a while, but he had been quite helpful the last time we'd battled together.

"I don't keep tabs on him, but he pops in every once in a while."

"Ah. Look!" I whispered after we'd wandered back into the tunnels. "Clarette was right."

There was, indeed, a cavernous ancient temple that looked classical in nature. Pre-Classical, even. The columns were short and squatty instead of long and elegant, and the pediments didn't boast any sculptures. Instead, I saw even older, Archaic elements and apotropaic motifs of fearful masks meant to turn away evil. Sadly, they seemed to have stopped working in this particular temple, because there were also Knights with their titanium armor and they radiated pure hate.

"What are they doing?"

"Nothing good," Blaise said grimly. His fingers flexed around his weapons as we watched the Knights sealing human-sized jars with hot wax, marking them with the Templar insignia, and putting them in neat rows. The pottery was painted in the red and black style of ancient Athens, although the scenes they portrayed were completely new. People arguing, fighting, slumping to the ground in despair. Others were more violent, including strangulation and decapitation. They were the worst home collection of decor I could have ever imagined.

"Those are Greek pithoi jars," Sophie told us, no doubt helped by her belt's knowledge.

Some sort of energy eddied around the center of the room. I felt a crackle of power and the metallic sting of sulfur. The pithoi jars were full of it. Raw, potent, unrefined power. One of the Knights paused to meet a woman at the edge of the temple, and a burst of electricity zapped through me as they began to kiss passionately.

"I know them," I whispered, not sure why I was so

shocked. "It's the fornicating couple from the graveyard I visited with Maman and again in the library at UFOPP. He's a Templar? I thought he was just a wannabe, looking for admission."

"So much for that vow of chastity. These Templar leaders are breaking their vows left and right."

Sophie couldn't tear her eyes off of the couple, but neither could I for that matter. "They seem to have a knack for such embraces in odd locations," she said.

With a bit of shock in my voice, I nodded at her belly, "She's pregnant!"

"Well, what did you expect?" Sophie asked, flipping her hair. "They were like bunnies. I guess they truly enjoy each other's bodies, and it is not a consummation for the greater good."

"I wonder if the baby was conceived over the warrior's grave, and if so, will the child truly have the powers of a warrior?"

"Anything is possible," Sophie said again. Apparently, it was her new motto. This was clearly the work of a certain polar bear shifter. Anything was, indeed, possible.

"Could we focus on the problem?" Blaise asked irritably.

"Sure. What, exactly, is the problem?"

Blaise opened his mouth and shut it. "I'm not sure. But it feels odd, doesn't it? Wait, they're doing something to the jars."

We crouched lower and watched as the couple took large paddles and stirred a mixture in the largest pithoi. An air of despair swirled around it. There was an odd surrasting sound, and it took me a few minutes to realize the noise was moans, soft moans inhaled and exhaled like lungs breathing in and out.

A woman in a Greek chiton much like Sophie's sat next

to the jar, her hands bound, her right leg attached to the jar. In a situation full of odd and downright weird things, the woman may have been the weirdest. Large pieces of her skin peeled off, perhaps from intense exposure to the toxic brew inside. Stranger still, the new skin underneath resembled clay in texture and color, making her an odd echo of the jars around her. Curls of black hair hung in perfect, glossy ringlets down her back, although they were bound away from her face by a silver circlet of pressed olive leaves. Her eyes were closed, and her hands limp in their binds. She seemed desolate... hopeless, even.

When the man lifted the wooden paddle, it came out dripping wet with a mossy black substance. "What is that?" I asked, and my companions shrugged.

Upon closer inspection, I could see tiny, pulsing spots of forest green. That was the source of the stench. Despite myself, I took a deeper whiff to study it. There was a sweet undercurrent with it. Too sweet, almost like the smell of overripe fruit and honeysuckle.

As quietly as possible, I snapped a few grainy pictures with my camera phone and sent them to Romaine with a big question mark underneath it. What was the point of kissing demons if they couldn't help you solve mysteries?

As if summoned by my own text, Blaise's phone vibrated. He answered it with a whisper and had a quick, muffled conversation. When he got off, he turned to us. "Anouk says there is a ship docking out a little way in the water."

"Et alors?" Sophie said. "There are lots of ships in the water."

"This one caught her attention."

"Why?" I asked.

"Because. Templars are loading jars in them. Ancient Greek jars."

22

"Any idea what they're doing with them?" I asked.

Blaise rubbed his chin. He'd seen a lot of strange things in his time. "Maybe, it's a biological weapon."

"Like anthrax?"

"A magical version, anyway. It's only a guess."

"Obviously," Sophie snarled. "Maybe it's some kind of potion they're putting in everyone's coffee. Maybe that's why we all feel like crap."

"Spoken like a true café owner," I said. "But that doesn't mean you're wrong."

My phone buzzed on my hip, making me practically jump. "Sorry. I'm a little skittish," I said, looking at the screen. "Whoa!"

Everyone waited, but I didn't expand. I couldn't. I was too shocked. Romaine's response stared at me in black and white—*Congratulations. You've found Pandora and her infamous box. More of a jar, though, isn't it?*—yet I still couldn't quite fathom it. Even more annoying, I could practically hear his chortle through the screen.

"What do we do?" I typed back.

"Your guess is as good as mine. Follow your instincts."

I rolled my eyes. Trust Romaine to be simultaneously complimentary, disarming, and useless.

When I looked up, Sophie and Blaise stood arms crossed, unified in their annoyance. "Care to clarify?" Sophie asked.

"Sorry. Romaine said it's Pandora's Box."

Sophie coughed. "Like THE Pandora?"

"Yes." I pointed at the woman. "Pan-dor-a."

"The name is from the Greek," Sophie said, a finger to her nose. "It means all-gifted, because the gods gave her many gifts before sending her away from Olympus. She's the Eve of ancient Greece."

Blaise scoffed. "That's impossible. An immortal on Earth that we haven't uncovered? Besides, how would Romaine know that?"

"Because he's a demon. A really powerful one. Who's been on earth for hundreds of years."

Blaise only blinked, as if he'd always sort of known deep down, but just needed it confirmed. "I knew there was something off about that guy."

"Oh really? So being a demon is what made him 'off'?" I said. "And does the name Naberius ring a bell? What about moi?"

"Fine. Maybe I just don't like Romaine. Does that make you feel better? Non, don't answer. Just tell us, did he say how to stop it?"

"No. He told me to follow my instincts."

The practical capitaine frowned.

Unlike Romaine, Sophie had plenty of ideas. "Obviously, if that's Pandora's Box, we have to follow the jars and see where the Templars are shipping them." Sophie had her hands on her hips, which meant on her belt, and she was glaring at us.

"No," I shook my head, "we're not doing this here."

"What?"

"A stare down."

"Yes, we are. We have to know where they're going and what they're doing with them."

"But the source is right there," I pointed out.

"And we know where it is. We can always come back. If we leave now, we can catch the last ferry back to Marseilles and rent a boat. Better yet, we can sneak aboard their boat."

"Headed toward possible hell!"

I went too far. With that, Sophie turned and headed topside to join the others. I hesitated. I hated leaving Pandora alone, but I also didn't have a plan, and now I didn't have my wing woman. "Fine," I finally said, "but this conversation isn't finished."

Outside, we quickly filled in the others.

Anouk understood the implications first. "You want us to follow murderous Knights with their boatload of precious cargo that was clearly designed to do nothing, and I mean absolutely nothing, good? I'm sorry, but that does not sound like a recipe for success." She had been chain smoking, if the cigarette butts surrounding her on the ground were any indication, although it was Clarette holding the cigarettes for her so she could focus on keeping her shirt in place.

"Yes," Sophie said in response, as if that one word answered all of Anouk's concerns.

"We can't leave," I insisted. "We can stop whatever is happening right here, right now."

Hortense shook her head. "I guarantee one thing. Whatever is happening here, it is only a cog in the machine. You slow down the machine, perhaps, but that alone does not break it."

I whirled around, desperation clawing at my throat. "Then why are you here, if that's what you really think?"

"I could ask the same of you. Why are you really here, Bernadette? We know what you really are, but do your friends know what you're capable of?"

"They know me," I said, feeling the slightest bit uncomfortable, shifting my weight from one side to the other.

"Not the whole you."

"We don't need to know anything more than what we see," Anouk said, her nose held high.

"Oh? Then you don't care to know the truth? That she is in your veins now, just like her mother is. She is in everything," Madame Hortense said, each word falling like an executioner's sword.

"I don't understand," Blaise and Anouk said in unison. Blaise more slowly, thoughtfully, while Anouk had a tinge of hysteria.

"Her blood is what created this new world order, just as your mother's original fall did the same so long ago. Didn't you ever understand what was happening with shifters and how they just... appeared?" Here, she snapped her fingers for effect, an echo of her old elegance returning. "It takes the stardust of falling stars to sprinkle their sulfuric powers over the land. But with Bernadette, literal drops of blood were flung across the planes of existence. Quoi? Don't believe me? Ask Romaine. He was there with you in the Infernal Regions, wasn't he?"

I nodded. There was no point in hiding it, but my mind was whirring. Templars, Pandora, the Order of the Ancients, my mother... didn't originally fall into my father's arms? It was too much! And Madame Hortense was relentless in her accusations.

"Romaine saw you attached to the mythical Golden Orrery, dripping blood across the skies, changing our world for the worst, ingratiating magic where once it was merely a whisper. Now, it is a scream."

"How do you know that?" I asked.

"Romaine didn't tell me, if that is what you are wondering. It is simple logic. This new world reeks of your blood. You forget, I know the ancient stories, meaning I know the only way such a transformation is possible. I am a student of ways to become immortal."

"Birdie!" Anouk's face had gone sheet white, her pupils dilated and large in the darkening evening. "You didn't say you were tortured."

My heart swelled; Anouk cared more about me being tortured than me unleashing untold amounts of my tainted blood, of magic, on the known world.

"Maybe a little," I said meekly, my entire self being exposed against my will.

A sob escaped from my throat, I couldn't stop it. My hand flew up to cover my mouth and then, Anouk crushed herself to me. "You're sitting down and we're taking a moment to gather ourselves. Alone." Anouk emphasized that last word, giving Madame Hortense a particularly poisonous glare. In the next moment, she ushered me to a rampart of weathered, yellowed stone to sit while she gave me a hug.

"Oh, Anouk. Mon Dieu. It's just all too much."

"We missed you, Birdie. I felt lost without you, honestly, I did. In such a little time, you've become the closest person in the world to me, more precious than I could have imagined. I will not stand to hear Madame Hortense try to make you feel bad. If you didn't want to tell us about the blood thing, then that's your right. It's not like you could have helped it by the sounds of it."

Another sob escaped. "I missed you, too. You know, as much as an unholy, halfling-demon can. I still can't believe it. I'm a demon. Maman wasn't human. Not even a little. There were lies built upon lies."

"She was a force, wasn't she?"

"I always thought she was odder than most French mothers, but I never really believed all that stuff about falling stars. It was too fantastical, too out of line with what she told me on a daily basis, that magic takes hard work and practice. Anyway, the only times she let talk of stars slip was after her lunchtime Bordeaux or when she got sick."

"She never brought it up otherwise?"

"Once a decade she would tell me the truth, and now I understand that she was testing me, trying to see if it triggered anything. So that's it. That's what she was hiding. She was a falling star, I'm a freaking demi-demon, and my stupid star blood is capable of ruining everything when it falls into the wrong hands. It's literally all my fault. I could have stayed right where I was and not try to find my father. I didn't even succeed. I found a shadow, a memory designed to trick me into coming to the Outer Planes."

"Hey, hey, it's okay. Shhh, don't cry, Bernadette," Anouk said, gently shushing me. "Plenty of humans are demonic enough without any help from being an actual demon, and I'd suspect plenty of other demons have human enough qualities. It's how you use them and what you let shine through that matters. Come now, you'll spoil your appetite. Shh, no more crying, cousin"

Just that word, *cousin*, was enough to send me into another spasm of shoulder shaking, sobbing tears. She still claimed me.

"Oh, Birdie. I have missed you, too," Anouk rocked me in her arms. "You know, as much one can miss an unholy, halfling-demon or demi-demon or whatever you call yourself that literally changes the fabric of our universe. Thanks for this, by the way." She nodded to her shirt strap that was trying to conga line down her arm.

I snorted up a tear, but I wasn't done being miserable yet. "I appreciate you not disowning me, but I do feel different now that I know. I want things I've never wanted before. I liked the feeling of Simon's fear, of making him feel small. It makes me wonder... was Maman like that? Was it not simply her French sensibilities being provoked when I wore my hair too long or too straight, but something worse? She was always a distant mother figure, cold even, but maybe it was her nature. Maybe it's my nature."

"Like what, Birdie? Are you trying to say your mother put people down because she liked to feed on their misery? That it invigorated her or nourished her? Even you, her own daughter? Your father, my uncle, mind you, didn't feel that way about her. He didn't see that at all, and she was great friends with my mother, Aenor. I never saw that, either. Look at how she acted with Amandine, especially at the end. She loved her family. She loved you."

I nodded. "I can feel that you truly believe that. It's a shift in the frequency of your vibrations. It was too subtle before but now I feel every shift like a jolt to my skin—Mon Dieu. Merde. Shit. Shit!"

"Birdie! What's wrong? Where are you going?" Anouk squeaked after me. "Birdie, wait!"

I was pacing, running my fingers through my hair,

muttering wildly under my breath. "There is no time to wait. I think I know what the Templars are doing."

23

"I think I know what they're doing, just not how they're actually going to do it."

"Well? Reveal all the answers you seem to possess," Madame Hortense said, still a little salty from not getting the reaction she wanted to her big reveal.

"Happily," I responded with equal annoyance. After all, who was she to reveal MY experiences to MY family and friends? That was my job.

"You can stop glaring," Madame Hortense said, "We're all waiting."

"The Templars are collecting and storing energy. Don't you see? Misery is caused by these evils they're releasing, and misery emits strong vibrations. Chaos vibrations. Those jars are full of the worst woes of life, which produces the most power."

"I thought everything already had vibrations, we were just un-attuned to them," Anouk fretted. "How can they be so powerful and strong now?"

"Because they were amplified when our world was remade," I winced as I said that, fully aware of why our realm had changed. "Before, I used to feel gentle vibrations, like a low-level massager kneading my consciousness. I could easily ignore them, especially from things like plants or rocks. Humans took a bit of practice, but Matthew's death helped me shut away anything magical. I was done with it because it hadn't saved him. Now, it's like a boombox pounding at my brain."

"Okay, so the vibrations are stronger now. What's that got to do with these jars?"

"The Templars are simply taking advantage of that change to make everyone even more miserable. They opened Pandora's Box and unleashed deeper, more potent versions of the seven evils to compliment the seven deadly sins. More misery experienced more intensely."

"But that would lead to wars, mass murder even," Sophie said as Madame Hortense's eyes glowed with realization.

"Exactly."

"But why?"

"To generate incredibly potent energy that they can harness. It's what they do. Think of all the magical items they've used over the years. They store energy in things, and they use them to achieve their ends."

Clarette's eyes were wide and her nose kept twitching. "Birdie, you're scaring me."

"I'm scaring me, too."

But it was Sophie's question that chilled us all to the bone. "If they're using the whole earth and all of humanity as a battery, then what are they trying to power, Bernadette?"

"I don't know. Something big, and the only lead we have so far are those jars." I pointed out to the harbor. "You were right, Sophie. We do need to follow them and see what they're up to, but we also need to stop the source of all this misery. We need to stop Pandora's Box here."

"Oh la," Anouk groaned. "I was really hoping the solution was something less life-threatening, like making a phone call. I could do that."

It wasn't like we had a lot of options before, and now the situation looked downright desolate.

"As I said before, this is only one cog," Madame Hortense said. "What are you going to do? Find and smash them all?"

I opened my mouth to reply, but surprisingly, Sophie beat me to it. "You know, from wearing this belt, I get bits and pieces of the other queens who dared to put it around their hips. There was one, a strong woman who was once a slave in the Caribbean based on the heat signatures I'm getting, who never promised to do anything more than save her people. She said she would be the touch that began the ripple. Even if we are only the touch, it will still send out a ripple, and ripples have the power to become tsunamis."

Madame Hortense eyed Sophie, her eyes slipping to the belt. If anything, she respected its power and its stored knowledge. She also respected anyone who could wear the belt, and Sophie certainly wore the crap out of it. Finally, Hortense nodded.

"Bon. Here's what we do." I said, bringing everyone's attention to me. "We're going to split up. Anouk, you and Clarette follow the jars. Find out where they're going. This is a recon mission only, Blaise's favorite type. That way, we'll be able to smash the next cog, as you so elegantly put it. Sophie, I think you should go with them to keep them safe, if necessary. The rest of us will be the touch that sets off the ripple, right here, right now."

"You're going to close Pandora's Box?" Sophie asked.

"If the creek don't rise," I said in English with a full Louisiana accent.

Blaise actually grimaced at that, but he also gave me a look that didn't require magic to read. He would support us to the end. He found the cause just.

"And what? We're just supposed to march back down there and instigate a raid?" Madame Hortense scoffed.

"That's exactly what we're going to do."

24

The deeper into the temple complex under the Chateau d'If we got, the more Templars we found. Men moved in simple white robes with pattée crosses emblazoned on their chests. They still wore their titanium vambraces, but not the full armor of a pitched battle. Behind them, their shadow demons capered, like grotesque versions of true shadows still learning how to follow. They'd morphed the place into a vast storeroom of jars and vats of hot wax to seal them. It was the world's most bizarre production assembly line.

A lone man stood at the top. He was one half of the fornicating couple, and I found it completely jarring to see him without the woman wrapped around his waist, and even more jarring to see a subordinate bow to him and call him Godfrey. On his index finger shone a bright, red jewel set in gold.

At that moment, he crouched next to the woman I now understood to be Pandora, the woman made of clay from ancient Greek mythology. The wife of the brother of Prometheus. The woman who was created to be a punishment for the gift of fire. A punishment in return for a gift. The gods wished to punish Prometheus so they gave his brother a wife and a jar they told her not to open under any circumstance and then filled her with Hermes' curious ways to ensure that she would. And thus, Pandora, like Eve, had to take the fall for why humans suffered. I thought about my shiny new word, *Ignis*, and how I wouldn't mind setting the patriarchy on fire for being so crappy.

Both her eyes and her hair were the color of dark honey. Her dress had been ripped up to her thigh, and her face was streaked with black dust. I had the feeling it was physically impossible for this first woman to cry. Water didn't mix with clay. Instead, her skin flaked off in large pieces that left rough patches beneath, like crocodile skin.

Blaise and Madame Hortense flanked me. It had been emotional saying goodbye to Anouk and Clarette and Sophie so soon after being reunited. I had kissed their cheeks, tear-stained cheeks in Anouk's case, and wished them luck. *Bonne chance.* Nobody wanted to separate, but we all had our parts to play to rid the world of one massive evil-sucking, magical threat.

"What do you think that ring is?" I asked. "Have either of you seen it before?"

Hortense's voice vibrated in a low growl. "I get the feeling it's not for fashion. You know, by the way it keeps lighting up and the sheer ugly audacity of it."

"That's the least of its oddness," I confirmed, thinking she sounded just like Sophie there. If they ever got over their differences, those two could actually be friends. "It's got all sorts of bad vibes and potent energy ripping off of it like a riptide. Remember the sapphire ring that Ashavan gave you, Blaise? Is it similar? Didn't that one hold a djinn?"

"Oui, which is why I gave it promptly to the Cathars."

"Of course you did."

"Yes. Protocol is protocol. Even in times of disaster or duress. Protocol is what separates us from—"

I moaned for him to stop. "Yes, yes, I get it. We're separating ourselves from them. Do you know if that ring holds a similar creature? He's wearing it, and it's lighting up, but he's not changing into a powerful djinn like when Ashavan activated his."

Madame Hortense held something to her eye. A mini-telescope. "Mon Dieu, that's because it's worse than that."

The hairs on the back of my neck prickled and stood on end. A primal response. "Worse? How can it be worse?"

"Because it holds all the demons in the world. Or, at least, it holds the power to control any of the world's demons."

"You mean..."

"That is Solomon's Seal. King Solomon. The Templars were said to have gained all of their power from black magic. It was one of the reasons used to persecute them."

I remembered Romaine telling me these rumors when we were in Juf. He'd said it was possible they'd found things when digging in Jerusalem that helped fuel their quick ascent—and quicker descent.

The implications of that statement had only just begun to reverberate when the man's head snapped toward our hiding spot. Instinctually, we ducked, but that probably made it worse.

I heard voices and boots scraping on marble. My mind began to race, knowing we only had a few seconds to act.

"Blaise, do you feel Naberius? His cover might be beneficial here."

"Yes, but I don't think it's a good idea for him to come with that ring."

"Then get your weapons ready. All of them," I said, looking directly at his meteoric blade. "We're going to need them."

Blaise gave me a nod, but I could tell by his eyes he didn't like the odds of our non-existent plan, which was fair enough. I hated the odds. Never tell me the odds.

"I'm going to lead him away," I whispered. "Get to Pandora and get her away from here." Before either of them could pull me down or stop me, I stood up as dramatically as I could. Which was to say, I wreathed myself in fire and shouted, "Hey!" Then I followed that with a string of French expletives insulting his manhood, his derriere, his hidey-hole, and his precious Templars.

The man, Godfrey, followed the sound of my voice. His eyes narrowed and his white Templar cloak rippled behind as he strode forward, arm bent at the elbow, his hand hovering over his vambrace. Mentally, I was transported to the conference room at UFOPP. Something evil was about to explode. If I remembered correctly from Juf, and I think I did, they would be tiny demons with jagged teeth, white as powdered lead, and with absolutely no regard for any type of life.

"Remember your salt bombs," Hortense advised before slipping away in the opposite direction of Blaise. Despite our grievances, I didn't like leaving her alone and exposed.

Yet, that concern evaporated a moment later. I watched as she muttered something under her breath and a demon went down with iron chains around its tiny neck. Not finished with the creature, she began swinging it above her head like a mace. With a sickening crunch, she took out a row of entirely too slow Templars. Then, with an elegant movement of her other hand, she depressed a bottle of perfume that must have held something nasty and noxious. A handful of demons collapsed mid-jump, their collective surprise frozen on their angry faces.

I turned away appreciatively. Clearly, she could handle herself.

Godfrey stood before me now, and from this proximity, the ring glowed brighter. It had a light that my eyes could see, but something else pulsed below the surface, almost like a living heart beat. That terrified me more than anything.

The man saw me studying the ring and smiled, an arrogant smile of someone who knows they have the upper hand, which he certainly did. No arguments there. Then a sudden thought struck me. Could I steal it? In the past, I'd been able to control the vibrations of others, slowing them down to the point where time stopped. For them, at least. Why couldn't I do the same to this crazy man? I'd freeze him, gently slip off the ring, and then unfreeze him. He'd still be there grinning like an arrogant idiot, completely unaware of the fact that I was now the biggest, baddest thing in the room.

It was a great plan. An amazing plan, in fact. Except, the ring resisted my every effort to slow it—and its wearer—down. No matter how hard I pushed, it pushed back harder. I didn't even know if Godfrey was aware or cared. He only knew that the ring made him impervious to my magic. Then, a really terrible thought popped into my mind, the reason why I failed.

Would Godfrey be able to control *me* with that ring? How easily? With a mere wave of his hand, a flick of his wrist? I prayed I was immune thanks to my father, fully aware of and fully ignoring the irony of it all.

Fine. Time to shift tactics, I told myself, trying to stay calm despite the panic building behind my navel. It didn't help that Godfrey was pulling his little shadow demons, all teeth and attitude, out of his pocket like the world's worst children's magician.

Think. Think. If I couldn't slow him down, maybe I could speed myself up. Yes, he had an army of shadow demons at his disposal and a ring that could potentially control me, but if he didn't know where to expect me... I wouldn't give him that chance.

I channeled the energy and the feel of the vibrations I'd pursued in the Room of the Unknown when I'd magically appeared from one place to another, a demon gift. I pushed *against* the molecules, forcing them apart, forcing them to let me through and slip from one place to another. I didn't want to go far. It wasn't like jumping from one realm to another. More like, from one spot in the room to another.

Again, a flash of blinding light, disorientation in the void, and then I popped into a new space only feet from where I began. Wobbling, I faltered a few steps before I gained my footing, like a sailor stepping off a boat. My heart, though, sang. I could be unstoppable. Birdie from the Bayou was long gone. She wouldn't even recognize me. She was still counting steps to the moon while I had journeyed far beyond.

The little maniacs with jagged teeth changed course, following my movement, but it was too late. I was next to Godfrey, just slightly behind him out of his range of vision.

His vibrations felt unnervingly fast, like his metabolism was working overtime. The Knight's head swiveled, a gasp escaping from his lips. He had no idea where I'd gone or what I'd done. Exactly as I hoped. I was the one who now had the element of sur—Arrgh!

In a move that was entirely too fast to have been made by Godfrey himself, his ringed hand was at my throat. He turned a moment later, his eyes furnaced with fire to match the ring's ruby intensity. "Ah, there you are." he said. "Did I forget to mention that the ring senses danger on its own accord? It comes in quite handy. Don't you think?"

A strangled sob escaped, but he squeezed harder, cutting off all air, and it wasn't just the physical attack. The ring pulsed with ethereal energy, an artifact of immense power. It nearly blinded me with its energy, and its touch seemed to burn.

I tried to stop myself, but I couldn't. The ring practically whispered to me all the forgotten knowledge of another realm, my home. Or at least Maman's. I stared too deep, I listened too long, and in that instant the world around me twisted and contorted, morphing into a grotesque visage of torment and despair.

The once familiar landscape of Chateau d'If dissolved, replaced by an infernal panorama. Ebony skies writhed with ravenous flames, casting a lurid glow upon the hellscape that stretched before my bewildered eyes. The ground beneath my feet transformed into obsidian rock, a testament to the eternal anguish that pervaded this forsaken realm. In the distance, demonic figures lurched and writhed, and anguished screams echoed through the fiery gusts. I felt dread tighten my heart as I realized where I was. Somehow, the ring had taken me back home, to Hell. A place I had never been and yet belonged.

The air was thick with acrid smoke, carrying the stench of burning sulfur and despair. Ghastly specters roamed the wasteland, their hollow eyes reflecting their pain. Their gaunt figures exuded hopelessness, their spectral whispers amplifying the weight of the desolation that hung in the air, a symphony of pain.

Time dissolved as I stood transfixed, a witness to the damning truth of my own existence. The ring had pulled back the tapestry of illusions, and I now beheld my own reflection in the charred mirrors of this infernal realm, a creature of darkness, born to sow chaos and despair.

And then it was gone, replaced with something that was, in its own way, worse—Godfrey's pitiless and pleased face as he studied my reaction. His yellowed teeth and rotten breath, like he didn't have dental hygiene in his neck of the woods, greeted me, making my eyes water even more.

"What did you see?" he asked. Then, he waved his ringed hand dismissively. "Never mind that. I have a better idea. Let's run an experiment, shall we?"

Without warning, the pressure eased. Godfrey threw me to the ground, and my elbows hit hard on the stone floor. I had no time to blink before my limbs turned to concrete, and I couldn't move, again.

His excitement, the mirth on his face, increased. "Ah, very good results. But this is science. We must run our tests again and again to be sure."

The ring flared once more, and my body jerked to a stand. It was true. He possessed Solomon's Ring. That was how the Templars were able to summon all of those demons to UFOPP's headquarters and take over the magical world. Take over me.

Godfrey clapped once, gleefully. "Oh, how wonderful. I have no idea what you could be. Surely not a high level demon, able to mask yourself as human? Your features are too perfectly plain, too human. Perhaps a siren? Hm, no. Too much gray in your hair. Well, that doesn't matter. It takes all types. What shall I have you do? Tie you up to a jar and dump your evil energy into it? Pandora, dear, would you like a friend to talk to?" he called over his shoulder.

Which was unfortunate, since that was when Blaise had chosen to attempt to untie the ancient Greek woman. To the capitaine's credit, he didn't freeze like a deer in the headlights as most would have, me included. He sprang into quicker action and began sawing away at her bonds. More than simple rope or twine held the woman, however, because he gained no traction.

Godfrey roared, spittle flinging everywhere, and a horde of jagged toothed demons rushed over my prone body, headed toward Pandora and Blaise.

I couldn't turn my head to see what was happening, and panic filled my veins like ice water. I heard a slice, like a stone cutting through paper, and knew he was using his meteoric blade. Still, he felt like the most vulnerable of us here, and this was going so horribly wrong. All I wanted was to walk in, crack open a jar, and flee. Not initiate a world war against an ancient order. That was for later, when we were more prepared. The moment Madame Hortense saw it was Solomon's Seal, I should have guessed I would be affected. I should have put a stop to our plan, regrouped, and thought of a new one.

It was the most helpless I'd ever felt, being controlled by Godfrey's ring. Not worse than the deaths of my family members, but the psychological factor of having no agency while my friends risked everything tore at my mind. Hopeless. That's what it felt like. Being hopeless. I wanted to throw protection around them, but I couldn't even say my own name without Godfrey's permission at the moment.

Hopelessness. A lack of...

Hope.

I recalled what I'd said to Anouk that first day back in

her apartment when the reality of this new horror show brought on by my blood and the warped magic of the Templars had welcomed me home, invaded my life.

Hope is all you need.

Maybe hope was all I had.

25

Jerusalem, 1307
  Knights Templar stronghold

JACQUES DE MOLAY *was too noble for his own good. If he wanted to let others bring down the Templars without raising an armored fist to save them, so be it. Godfrey would find a way around the Grand Master. It would not be subtle, and it would not be pretty; it would not even save their immortal souls, but Godfrey was beyond saving souls. He looked to immortality itself.*

Under the cover of a peasant's cloak, Godfrey swept through the tunnels of the temple, ancient already by the first of the holy crusades. This was his very own holy crusade, unbeknownst to his sworn brothers.

At the thought of his brothers in faith, something much like guilt flared up, and Godfrey had to push it down, tuck it away, hide it behind his zealous beliefs. Was Solomon not holy? Was Solomon not wise? His very ring cavorted with demons, leaving all of them he met under his control, and no one claimed he was blasphemous. No, what Godfrey did here and now was not unholy. Not in the slightest. If anything, he was emulating the great king.

The most sacred of their treasures, found under the temple, remained in an unadorned shrine. The Templars professed poverty, lived simply, slept little, ate less. It was only proper to keep what they'd excavated as simply as they could, but the things they'd found were too precious to entrust to any mortal man whose whims were known to change with the breeze. To keep such sacred treasures was a conundrum, to be sure, but it seemed Jacques de Molay, 23rd Grand Master, and soon to be the last, had finally decided. They would give it all up, and with their treasures, their lives. Just to be godly enough to save their pitiful souls.

As he crept through the tunnels, the clash of swords and their screams had already begun. Godfrey could hear his brothers being rounded up, beaten, flogged; he could imagine their blood streaming down their cheeks and stinging their eyes. This was no Judas act; if they could ask Godfrey, see into his heart, they would understand he was not betraying them. He was saving them. He was giving the Templars a future.

His fingers shaking uncontrollably, Godfrey fumbled open the reliquary where Solomon's infamous seal lay on a simple cloth cushion. It needed no adornment, just like the Templars and Godfrey himself. Now, his hands truly were uncontrollable, and it took a few tries to jam the ring on his forefinger. The screams were worse now, growing louder. He hardly had to imagine the blood soaked corridors he'd have to scramble back through. Already the tang of it thickened the air around him.

If their enemies claimed the Templars worshiped Baphomet, more than a demon, a deity, then why prove them wrong? Why not embrace it? Why not prove them... right? In doing so, Godfrey would save their entire existence from the flames of the pyre.

All at once, Godfrey's head snapped back on his neck. The power soaked from his fingers to his toes. There was a seductive whisper, the stench of sulfur. A subtle shift in movement that hadn't been there before... and then, darkness. Cold darkness.

Godfrey's laugh reminded me of the Egyptian immortals who had lost their grip on sanity a long time ago. He seemed like he was at the beginning stages, kept alive by the power siphoned through the ring, no doubt. I bet he couldn't bear to take that thing off. This was a febrile man, all chaotic, nervous energy.

He twisted my face and ground my nose in the ground like a bad puppy. I wanted to scream at him, *That's not how you train a puppy, you sick bastard!*, but I couldn't. He had my body under his complete control.

My body, but not my soul.

He controlled my demon side, but I hated to break it to him, I had multiple personalities. Actually, that was a lie; I couldn't wait to break it to him. My human side was positively itching to gouge out his eyeballs. Did that sound demonic? Nope, it was pure-hearted revenge for all of the horrible headlines and misery he was creating here. And revenge was a very human trait.

I heard more ripping sounds as Blaise tore through demons like paper and then his Sig-Sauer fired. I counted fifteen rounds. In between shots, I caught the distinctive pop of the salt bombs and heard the clank of armor. Together, they told me that Blaise and Madame Hortense were holding their own. Godfrey gave an annoyed grunt and left me lying on the ground.

I tried clenching my fists, staggering to my knees, anything to get my human side to take over. Whatever the Seal did, Godfrey clearly had a powerful grip on my demonic half with it and it kept me tethered to the ground like a bad demon dog.

As a child when I was scared, I would picture myself in my favorite spot, safe and protected. I tried that now. I pictured myself on the beach not far from my childhood home in Louisiana. Out among the waves, shadowy tendrils writhed and clawed, but in the distance a flickering flame danced, pushing back against the darkness. Like Prometheus gifting humans fire, it held that spark of humanity.

Both sides called to me, but I chose the fire. I knew my answer lay there. As I walked in my mind, I called upon the knowledge and experiences acquired during my fifty years on Earth, the memories of empathy and compassion. The relationships I had built. The friendships, the family found and given. I saw my Amandine as a baby snuggled in my arms, mewing like a kitten. I remembered my wedding day, holding the train of my dress high as I stood under an umbrella, letting the rain come, letting the water slosh over my rubber boots, letting myself revel in the sudden spring storm and mother nature. Maman had scolded me for putting them on, but I hadn't cared. My feet stayed dry and I got some marvelous pictures. I pictured Maman, her hand on mine at the end.

I clung to these fragments, embracing them with a

newfound urgency as I stepped into the light. The fire roared now, a gravitational force drawing everything into its orbit, echoes of laughter and love. Humanity was not a burden, a weakness to be discarded, but a beacon of hope to be cherished.

When I returned to the scene, I found myself standing, and I had full control of my body. Did that make me fully human in that moment? Or had my human side simply taken the controls? I didn't know, and I didn't care. All that mattered was that I was free of that infernal ring's orbit.

Godfrey stood before me raining holy hell down on the room. He had his back to me and his hands up, the ring glowing so red that I worried it might melt. Demons were literally coming out of the walls. They simply climbed out between crevices and dropped from the ceiling. Two had attached themselves to Blaise's leg, another to his back. He writhed in pain. Madame Hortense stood at the top of a metal structure, frantically pumping her perfume bottle at the hordes below.

My presence didn't even register with Godfrey. He was so used to having total control over demons that he never considered the possibility that I might get free. There was only one tiny problem; I couldn't use magic. If I did, the ring would neutralize me faster than I could act.

But I didn't exactly need magic, standing where I was. All I needed was my foot and a nice-sized brick. With one big step, I ninja kicked Godfrey in the balls, human-style. He crumpled and I clocked him over the head. He rolled over with a grunt, his own consciousness flickering out for the moment.

With no one giving it orders, the ring suddenly went dark. I could still feel the power radiating off of it, but it no longer actively called forth new demons. That didn't mean the demons onsite relented. The scene was already too chaotic, the demons hunting for blood. More piled onto Blaise, who cried out in agony as one bit his arm.

"Ah, screw it," I said out loud. Even if it felt good to fully embrace my human side for a moment, that didn't mean I wanted to give up the demon in me. I'd seen enough from my brushes with demons to know there was good there too, and certain things came in useful.

I closed my eyes and returned to my beach. This time, I let in thoughts of Romaine and Naberius, too. He sat on my shoulder cawing. "Yes, yes, I see you too," I said, and he nuzzled my ear. With so much love to pull from, even demonic love, I felt supercharged. Yes, demons were capable of emotions. Of love. Of protection. It was why ancient societies used to keep demons on their doors, to protect them from other demons. I used that now.

"*AN.BAR šá-kin!*" I bellowed.

Chains shot off in every direction, and instantly, half the demons in the room were held fast in place. A few Knights Templars became enmeshed as well. Yet, even those who escaped the chains froze, suddenly aware that I was now in control of the situation. Finally, I was the biggest and baddest thing around. And it felt amazing.

I cleared my throat. "The ring has been neutralized. This temple is no longer under Templar control. Demons, I'll give you one minute to decide what you want to..." I went silent as the tiny concussion of hundreds of demons fleeing back home broke up my speech. And people said demons were mindless little things!

When they were all gone, I turned to the Templars. "Drop your weapons, and you will be spared."

My demand was met with a collective clang of weapons hitting the ground. So, they weren't so zealous that they'd give up their lives so easily. Maybe there was hope for humanity after all. It was a simple matter of Madame Hortense tying them up and Blaise calling in his Cathar bosses to bring them to some sort of honest and fair justice.

Blaise stood next to me, tending to his wounds. His face wore a determined expression, but when I got close enough, he paused, blood dripping onto the floor in steady dots like Morse Code, but I didn't need to decipher them. His arms were wide open. I let him fold me into a hug.

I stood in Blaise's warm embrace for a long time, tears running down my face, letting all of the emotions from the last thirty minutes slobber on his sleeve. Like a good soldier, he held me in place, never wavering.

After a minute, I even felt a pat on my back. "You did fine," I heard Madame Hortense announce. "I don't know how a demon could succeed against Solomon's Seal, but it worked. You did it."

I ran the back of my sleeve across my nose, trying to clean up as best I could. "I found my humanity, and focused on that. The ring couldn't touch me there."

Madame Hortense nodded appreciatively. "You are quite surprising, Bernadette. Maybe you are worthy of the Sisterhood after all."

I ignored that last part. Neither I, nor Madame Hortense understood why I could see the ouroboros, but I could only handle so many mysteries in one day.

Below me, I heard Godfrey stir the tiniest bit and I slipped off the ring before he got a chance to cause more problems. "Arrest him or something, would you?" I said to Blaise, waving my hands in his direction, remembering Simon's death and knowing I could do something different here. Hopefully something better.

"Avec plaisir, Madame," Blaise replied, but without the

sustaining power of the ring, Godfrey's body had begun to do something... gross. It began to shrivel and bubble, turning to goo before our eyes.

Blaise hesitated, his heightened sense of duty forcing him to still look for a way to capture him and lead him to what was left of UFOPP or the Cathars.

"Give it up, Capitaine," Madame Hortense pronounced. "You cannot put handcuffs on slime."

My eyes re-filled with tears. Even when I didn't mean to, I still did harm.

Blaise took me back in his arms. "It's okay. You couldn't have known that was going to happen."

"But maybe some part of me did. Maybe I wanted him to die. Maybe, no matter what I think, I'll always be a demon. My subconscious might be stronger than anything else."

"If that was the case, you never would've broken free of the curse. This was his own fault. He wore the ring, knowing the consequences, and leaving the ring on his finger wasn't an option."

I snorted a glob of snot and nodded. It was true. Godfrey had left us no choice but to remove the ring. "I'm just glad it's over," I said.

"It's not over," he replied, snapping back into capitaine-mode.

I followed his finger to the woman tied to a jar.

The woman slumped in her ties, all the blood drained from her fingers and hands that were held tight above her head. Her head lolled on her neck. She looked nearly dead and was brittle to the touch. The whole scene made me furious, at the gods and their arrogance, and at the Templars and their power hungry ideals. No one should have to go through with this.

"Excuse me, Pandora? You are Pandora of the Box or jar or pithoi or whatever, right?"

The woman stared at me, her eyes barely seeing.

Madame Hortense knelt down and studied the bonds. "We have to figure out how to free her, and then we have to figure out how to close the jar. Even if the Templars can't store it anymore for... whatever it was they were doing, this thing is still spewing misery into the world like a noxious gas."

I knew she was right. It made me physically ill to stand next to the jar, the fumes pouring from the crack, and it was awful enough to make me feel it all. Anxious, angry, help-less. You name it, the jar amplified it. It felt like a million spiders crawling on my soul... while drowning in the darkest, deepest part of the ocean... with my hands tied behind my back.

Madame Hortense's mouth moved and her face flickered as she concentrated on the knot holding Pandora in place. Her magic always smelled sweet and sickly, a mixture of the beautiful perfumes she produced and the darkness she had lived through. The cords blazed, but they didn't budge.

"I need help," she gasped.

"I'm trying," I called back, tugging at the lines, not sure what else to do. "How can we untie you?" I asked the woman, my voice rising in equal proportion to my anxiety. My fingers pulled uselessly at the ropes that bound her with more than simple fibers.

"Open the jar," she said, faintly. "Let it out."

"You are Pandora, then?"

"That was not my name. I was Anesidora. She Who Sends Up Gifts. Pandora is a corruption of my purpose. Yes, they gave me gifts, but I had others."

"You had other gifts to give?" In the back of my mind, I thought that's what we all wanted for ourselves. To know as women, even if we stayed at home or went into the workforce, we had more gifts to give; more things to offer the world. "Could you maybe give me the gift of knowing what to do in this case?" I asked.

"Hope is all you need."

"I know, I know, but I was hoping for something a little practical."

"Hope is all you need," she repeated, her eyes drooping almost shut.

Then it came to me. She meant it literally. Hope. That was what was left in the jar! Sometimes, spending a lot of time around Anouk came in handy.

After the last ten minutes, I knew I could work with hope, but I wasn't sure how in this case. Hope sounded great, but a whole lot of misery was about to come with it. Did one outweigh the other? Would it be enough to be the ripple that begins the tidal wave or would it simply drown us in terrifyingly reckless hope?

Yet we simply had to win, and not even the hopeless fight as hard as those that believe in their team—those that are fighting for love.

"What happens to you if I let out hope?"

Pandora's eyes blinked open a slit. "I will go with it."

It felt like my own arrow pierced my heart. "What? I can't do that."

"It has been too long here, forced to do the bidding of everyone and anyone who finds me. I am ready to be dust. To be one with the earth from which I was created. Let me go."

"Hurry up, Bernadette," Hortense snapped.

Her honeyed eyes asked for no mercy. She wouldn't know what to do with it. Her request was simple, so I opened the jar.

The air vibrated at a different frequency. I could physically feel it, like a sonic boom that makes you take a step back and shakes your bones. It was intense and hard to hold onto. Then it really started. A torrent of darkness surged forth, a malevolent force fully unleashed, tearing at the very fabric of existence. Screams and afflictions, dormant for ages, sliced past my eyes.

The intensity of the ills inside made me double over. Disease, with its insidious tendrils, crept along the ground, its touch spreading a vile contagion. War, a tempest of fury, stormed through the air, raining down destruction. Greed, a ravenous beast, devoured compassion and empathy, leaving only the hunger for more. Famine, unsated and unrelenting, took the fruits of the land for itself, took more than it needed. It was a parade of suffering the likes of which I'd never seen or experienced before, not even in my vision.

"What have we done?" I screamed to cover the vacuum.

I could see in Madame Hortense's terrified eyes that she agreed. This woman had seen enough to fill a hundred lifetimes, and yet, nothing had prepared her for this. We both lunged for the cover, ready to reseal the jar, but a coarse hand steadied us.

"We are almost there," Pandora said.

And then it was done. The jar was empty and the world felt sick, sicker than when we had begun. The de-fanged Templar Knights wailed in the distance, prisoners of their own curse. It was the only silver lining that I could see in our decision.

Or, was that an actual light? It was faint, I couldn't be sure, but I thought the jar was... glowing.

"Here it comes," Pandora said. "The last gift. Hope."

I waited, my breath held, as if a sudden movement would cause it to flee or to return to the depths of this cursed jar.

"Some have thought that it, too, was meant to be an evil. False dreams to keep humans from ever being too motivated, but that's because the gods didn't understand its power. It was too fleeting for them to grasp. They thought hope was weak, yet it has always been the most powerful thing in the jar."

A moment later, a small light peeked out. It looked almost mammalian as it crawled over and curled itself around Pandora's neck. "Hello, old friend," she said. "It is time to undo the damage."

As she spoke, she began to disintegrate, like a dandelion

blown to the wind. Bright pieces of her began to swirl through the air, disappearing into the ether, but they weren't alone. I could feel the ills following her, heeding her call. Her pithoi cracked, too, and all around us, the world began to rumble and moan as an ancient relic of immense power finally began breaking down.

The Templar jars closest to us went first. The seals sizzled and they began to smoke, releasing their ills, not into the world, but dissipating into nothingness. Then, the jars stacked in rows along the back wall began to vibrate, the world's most dangerous storage bin being robbed of its power.

"Is that..." I strained my ear.

"Singing," Blaise finished. "It's coming from the town. It must be deafening to reach us here."

Merely letting out hope didn't have the power to undo the magic of my blood, to return the world to its former state, but it undid the sting of the transformation. Without the Templars pouring misery into the world, things became bearable, and one by one, the Knights stopped crying. Their curse was finished.

We climbed to the surface and watched the people of Marseilles dance and light off fireworks in the distance. We had done this, and maybe we would someday look back and see tonight as the beginning of a great transformation. Maybe we would make the world whole, perhaps even better. That was called hope.

I felt my phone buzz. "Hello, cousin," I answered.

"Oh, good, you're not dead."

"Merci. The feeling is mutual."

"What happened?" she asked. "We felt a shift."

"The first ripple has been sent."

"Great! What does that mean exactly?"

"Pandora, I mean Anesidora, went home, and she took her miseries with her."

"All of them?"

"As far as I can tell."

"I feel amazing." Anouk announced. Then, after a moment, she added, "Do you think Romaine will still hold up his end of the bargain?"

"You mean, will he find you a handsome and horny man to help distract you from your earthly cage? Yeah, I think he will do that."

"Good."

"So, it wasn't the curse?" I asked. "You're still interested?"

"The curse just amplified what was simmering under my skin for too long. It's time I get back out there."

"That too, is good. Where are you?"

"In the middle of the Mediterranean Sea. Most of the jars disintegrated, and the crew is running around losing their minds, but it's already clear where they were headed."

"Where?"

"To the Holy Land. And, based on my calculations, to a very specific part. Jerusalem."

"That's where Solomon was, where the Templars were. They're basing themselves in their old hub of power."

"How?" Anouk fretted. "Jerusalem, and the world, is a lot smaller than it used to be. They can't hide forever in a city like that."

"They have new tools at their disposal, and, I'm sorry to say, my blood helps that. It's why Simon wanted me there in the shadow realm. He wanted my blood and for this to happen." I also remembered the unbreakable net filled with things I could only dream about. "This is about to get a whole lot bigger."

To be continued...

Thank you so much for continuing to fly with Birdie. It's only going to get more exciting now that we've pushed into the Outer Planes. To continue to help Birdie to fly, your reviews are the most important thing you can do, besides good old-fashioned word of mouth. Please consider leaving one here for DATING MIDLIFE DEMONS!

Of course, don't forget to pre-order for a dollar discount! CURSING MIDLIFE DEMONS will be out in the New Year. Is that cover epic or what? Blurb coming soon!

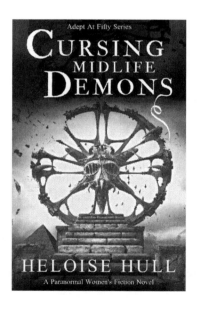

AUTHOR'S NOTE

Author's Note:

Here are your historical notes on the book! I hope you enjoy the history behind the fantasy as much as I do, as I attempt to weave it all together in a cohesive way like one of Athena's tapestries.

The fight in the grotto with Nimue was based on Beowulf's fight with Grendel's mother. Read it (and hear it!) in Anglo-Saxon here: Beowulf for Beginners - The Fight at the Mere

For Karnak's Holy of Holies, you can see it with Rick Steves here: Luxor Temple, Religious Capital of Ancient Egypt | Rick Steves Classroom Europe

The festival in Nefertiti's chapter is based off of the parade held by the first Ptolemaic pharaoh, Cleopatra's ancestor. Completely different time period, but still, ostentatiously gorgeous. And that controversial theory that it was two of Nefertiti's daughters who held the throne, the first and only co-female pharaohs in history, is actually a real theory being proposed in this, the year of our Lord 2023.

Enjoy! King Tut's Sisters Took the Throne Before He Did, Controversial Claim Says | Live Science

I had this crazy idea after researching the obsidian mirror for book 3, CROSSING MIDLIFE DEMONS, that John Dee was up to a lot of occult no good back in his day. I'd also read about some "angelic" language he'd discovered. A few months into writing this book, I discovered the Voynich manuscript. I thought, is it possible that Dee... no. Maybe? Did he get conned by his friend, Edward Kelly, whom he was working with on the language? It turns out, I'm not the first to connect those dots. Read about the possible connection here. The Voynich Manuscript | Research | The Guardian and see images of the mirror at the British Museum.

For those interested in the name Anesidora as opposed to Pandora, please see the white ground kylix at the British Museum.

The "gifts" bestowed on Pandora came as quotes from Hesiod's Works and Days, lines 60-105.

As always, thank you for reading. It truly means the world and all of the Outer Planes to me.

ALSO BY HELOISE HULL

Forty is Fabulous:

Making Midlife Magic

Making Midlife Madness

Making Midlife Mistakes

Making Midlife Marvels

The Hades and Persephone Duet: A Fantasy Romance:

Of Thorns and Bones

Of Flames and Thrones

Adept at Fifty

Chasing Midlife Demons

Slaying Midlife Demons

Crossing Midlife Demons

Dating Midlife Demons

ABOUT THE AUTHOR

Unlike her namesake of medieval infamy, Heloise doesn't intend to have her midlife crisis in a nunnery. She'd much rather drink espresso martinis and chant in fairy rings while wearing socially questionable clothing.

In her other pen names, Heloise writes romance, nonfiction, and epic fantasy with tinges of the ancient world all thanks to dual degrees in archaeology and Classics. She splits her time between St. Louis and Chicago with her husband, two kids, and ~~two~~ one cat, and is too heartbroken to plot how to bring in a puppy for the moment. Hug your real babies and your fur babies.

Manufactured by Amazon.ca
Bolton, ON